THE CRANES THAT BUILD THE CRANES

JEREMY DYSON

ILLUSTRATIONS BY HANNAH BERRY

ABACUS

First published in Great Britain in 2009 by Little, Brown
This paperback edition published in 2010 by Abacus

A CIP catalogue record for this book
is available from the British Library.

ISBN 978-0-349-12096-6

Illustrations copyright © Hannah Berry 2009

Earlier versions of 'Out of Bounds', 'The Coué', 'Come April'
and 'Michael' appeared in the *Guardian*, *Phobic*, *Big Night Out*
and *The Book of Leeds* respectively.

Typeset in Caslon by M Rules
Printed and bound in Great Britain by
Clays Ltd, St Ives plc

Papers used by Abacus are natural, renewable and
recyclable products sourced from well-managed forests and certified
in accordance with the rules of the Forest Stewardship Council.

Mixed Sources
Product group from well-managed
forests and other controlled sources
www.fsc.org Cert no. SGS-COC-004081
© 1996 Forest Stewardship Council

Abacus
An imprint of
Little, Brown Book Group
100 Victoria Embankment
London EC4Y 0DY

An Hachette UK Company
www.hachette.co.uk

www.littlebrown.co.uk

For Nicky – the crane that builds my crane

Contents

Isle of the Wolf

David Spotpal had a secret and that secret was fear. It was primal and it came in the dark.

Spotpal was a very wealthy man, though this hadn't always been the case. He was an estate agent and now a property developer, with an impressively broad portfolio. He had begun by selling on ex-council houses in the mid-eighties, at first in Archway where he had grown up and then gradually spreading out to Tufnell Park, Camden and Kentish Town. In a supernaturally short span of time – or so it seemed to his competitors – he had diversified into commercial properties. Office blocks, industrial units, warehouses – initially on Greater London's uglier shores lapped by the orbital grimness of the M25 and then closer and closer to the more desirable islands of the West End and the City. From here it was a short leap to ever more exotic and remunerative markets overseas. Now his empire encompassed a wide range of developing and richly profitable locations in China, North Africa and Dubai. Places whose names he had not even heard of as a child. The idea that he would regularly fly to these distant lands business class . . . well, in his youth just to be aboard a plane was to be in the province of kings, princes and international football players. Then money had been an absence, a clutching terror. Now it was an ocean – a freshwater ocean at that – where one could drink and drink and drink and know that one would never be dry again. The ease with which this had happened was as mysterious to Spotpal as it was to his rivals.

Regardless of this material success Spotpal had not had a peaceful night's sleep since his early childhood. It was not the supernatural that he feared but the evil that lay inside other men. He had a brief, barely retrievable memory of a comfortable small room, patterns of repeating brown monkeys lining the blue wallpaper. But this was mostly obliterated by another, intense, pounding recollection of something harsh and cold that hurt and never stopped hurting. A ground-floor room and a small mattress on the floor. It was cold and the air was wet with damp. It smelled of wet bricks and earth and when he slept his head was level with the pavement outside. He would hear footsteps approaching from two hundred metres away and receding as they passed. And because the flat was only two doors down from a blood-brown brick-walled pub with metal grates over its windows, weekend nights were broken by the sound of fights and shouts and screams that seemed to be in the room, inches from Spotpal's face. At some point the bedroom lost its door. From then on it remained permanently open to the dark corridor outside. Spotpal would lie there, waiting for the morning, without a watch or clock to guide him through the hours, willing the soft light to creep along the floor from the lone mesh-embedded window high in the damp-scarred wall beyond. Why the memory hurt so much it was hard to say. He could find no injury to accompany it, other than a dark sense of things not being good with his tired and often absent mother. But the feeling of groundlessness, of being held suspended over an unfathomable pit, never left him, and in his teenage years it found a correlate in the possibility of random violence which he began to experience around him – the stabbings, the beatings, the occasional murders. Although one of these had yet to claim him, Spotpal was sure in his heart that it was simply a matter of ill luck and unavoidable circumstance before this happened. Death lurked and it would take him soon.

When his business began to make notable profits Spotpal started to indulge himself. Not on the cars, or drugs, or tailored suits that others in his trade seemed to enjoy, but on domestic security. After one particularly large dividend he telephoned a company called Gramscis which had a large premises on the Holloway Road and arranged for a consultation. The anticipation he felt waiting for the representative to come round would not have been keener had he been expecting a high-class escort. His flat was on the third floor of a serviced block near Old Street, with a reception that was manned twenty-four hours a day, so one might have thought that there was little need for any extra protection. Nevertheless Spotpal spent nearly a thousand pounds on deadlocks, hinge bolts, Banham gates and night latches in a single cash purchase. For a while this felt like the most satisfying expenditure he had ever made. But only for a while.

Several weeks after the devices' installation Spotpal found his imagination worrying a way through what he had believed to be impregnable. Intruders with power tools modified for near-silent operation drilling out his keyholes, lock-pickers with the prowess of Las Vegas conjurers, psychotic trespassers with near-supernatural skills of forced entry – all began to queue on the fringes of sleep to perpetuate his state of disquiet. He started at every noise and woke unrested in the morning. He began to scour specialist literature and trade journals for the latest in home protection equipment. Soon the locks were joined by closed-circuit televisions, monitored burglar alarms and rolling shutters on internal doors. The compulsion to protect himself had flowered into full obsession.

As Spotpal's personal fortune rose, the means to feed this obsession expanded too. And of course his increasing wealth exposed him to those who might covet it. He moved to a detached residence in East Finchley – formerly inhabited by an importer and distributor of fruit machines. The house was surrounded by a double-perimeter, three-metre fence, each rung of which was topped with a sharpened and polished point. When the gate was shut the place was as impregnable as a moated castle. And indeed relief came on his first night in the property. Until the third week, when Spotpal's newly acquired sense of security was routed by an imaginary pair of villains equipped with nothing more than a set of window-cleaner's ladders.

The next stage was one he had considered some time before, but had avoided because he was aware, uncomfortably so, that it pushed him beyond the boundaries of what might be considered normal. Nevertheless the lack of peace and security he was experiencing on a now-nightly basis led him to the decision. He employed a full-time bodyguard. This involved some elaboration of the truth. He felt the need to embellish his circumstances to the agency so that they would take his need seriously. He explained that his dealings overseas had brought him into contact with some unsavoury characters who had been inadvertently upset by some of his transactions – now he needed to protect himself, at least until the storm died down. The agent listened patiently and sympathetically to Spotpal's fictions. He assured his prospective client that he understood his position and that they would be able to provide close protection of the most discreet yet reliable nature. And when Spotpal met Danny Rowe – the ex-marine and middleweight wrestler assigned to him – he experienced a new kind of solace. That this man might be with him, keeping watch as he slept – well, this was everything he had been waiting for. For a time he imagined what it must be like to be Danny Rowe – huge, self-contained, confident that he could repel any aggression that might be directed towards him. At first the man was taciturn, but after some weeks they began to come to know each other. Rowe spoke of his experiences in the ring – fights where he felt so much pain that he did not know how he would endure the next minute. He explained how he developed an inner feeling to overcome the resistance. Pain was merely a steep hill to be climbed. It felt like it would go on and on and on, but there would always be a summit. There was no hill on earth without a summit. And from there on in the journey was always downhill.

Yet once again Spotpal found this period of peace, of nocturnal security, to be short-lived. Rowe's previous employment had been as a nightclub bouncer in Ilford and he had made enemies of a local gang of sub-Yardie dealers. He was accosted outside his house and beaten with an iron bar. He lay comatose in a hospital for three weeks before he died. A shattered Spotpal felt the loss personally. He attended Rowe's funeral and wept – wept at the persistence of his own unending torment.

And it continued as the years passed. He experimented with drugs – temporary suicide on a recurring basis – but they made him feel sick and faded and weak so he gave them up. He had an alcoholic period in the mid-nineties but he put on weight and didn't like looking at himself in the mirror, or in the changing room at the gym. Time spent seeing a psychotherapist – something maybe he should have tried sooner – was not productive – endless chat about a childhood he could not remember and did not want to remember. He needed to live in the now, act in the now, end this in the now. And as a new century dawned he received the resources with which he could surely do so and find the peace he craved.

The business sold for a very, very large amount of money. He could invest the capital and live off the interest without ever having to think about money again. And there was more. Equity that he had invested in the early eighties – mutual funds that were now coming to fruition. Interest that had compounded and then compounded again. In short David Spotpal was one of the wealthiest men in the country.

He first saw the island on a television programme. It was tiny. It barely figured on any maps. It lay midway between Corsica and France. It had been privately owned for many years by the Giafferi family – descendants of Luigi Giafferi, the Corsican nationalist, and now they were seeking to sell. Naturally they wished to achieve the highest possible price and Spotpal did not disappoint them. It wasn't just the fact that the island was available for purchase that inspired Spotpal to act – its essential geography was a bigger part of its unique appeal. For Lalouppe – a pretty name that did not suit its aspect – was virtually a natural sea fort. Its coastline – not three miles in diameter – comprised jagged rock formations, sheer cliffs and a near-impossible approach from its northernmost tip. Only a skilled sailor in a small craft would be able to make the landing. The island was also unique in being an independent principality by decree of the Corsican constitution. Whoever bought Lalouppe would become ruler of what would be in effect his own country, subject to his own laws and his own sovereignty. This was Spotpal's logic: whatever his imagination might create – whatever torments and tortures, whatever the nightly parade of psychotics queuing to attack, to torture, to maim, just out of view in the darkness – would simply dissolve when faced with the brute fact that *it was not possible for them to come there*. There was no way – because physics and geography and the laws of nature meant that there could be no intruders on the island. And he would make this so by taking the natural fortification and enhancing it. He would commission and construct the most complete security system that had ever been constructed for a domestic dwelling. The goal was simple: to create a state such that when he was lying in bed awaiting sleep he would know – with absolute certainty – that he was safe from all possible harm. Around the time that he had made this decision an element of synchronicity came into play. An article in a trade journal – which Spotpal still took a subscription to – detailed the rise of a maverick Austrian architect called Franz Fenster. The man was already notorious for undertaking the design of a film studio – the largest and most elaborate ever built – for North Korean President Kim Il-Sung. But

Fenster's passion for detail, his vision and enthusiasm, and his taste for the unusual immediately made him the perfect candidate to fulfil Spotpal's vision. And vision it was. Spotpal felt it deep within him, in his gut, in his essence. It was something he was waiting for – had been waiting for all his life. Like Rodin searching for the sculpture in the marble, it was only a question of carving it out in actuality. Spotpal was not a cultured man – he had little interest in art or poetry – but had he done so he would have recognised that the thing he was striving to bring into being and the keenness with which he felt it – the clarity of the idea, the need to make it manifest around him – this was indeed the stuff of art. Lalouppe would be a hymn to home security – a monument to the protection of the self.

And so a meeting was arranged with Fenster and the commission set in motion.

'Please – so I may understand you – are your family to accompany you?' said the dapper gentleman sitting opposite Spotpal in the Savoy Grill. His look was eccentric and particular – a porkpie hat which he had not removed, a button-down Ben Sherman shirt and a small, delicately-trimmed pencil moustache. Bizarrely – and perhaps unintentionally – he resembled Kevin Rowland, the singer from Dexy's Midnight Runners.

'I have no family.' Spotpal's response was curt. He did not elaborate.

'And do you wish – how can I best express this – is there a time in the future when you will wish to play host to children?' Fenster smiled. Spotpal did not smile back.

'No,' was all he said.

'Excellent,' said Fenster. He smiled again and his pencil moustache seemed to expand, wriggling across his face. 'Then we can really go to work.'

In August 2001 a series of Sikorsky S-61 helicopters began their cycle of landing on and taking off from the warm but wind-battered plateau of Lalouppe's surface. They delivered building materials – concrete hardcore, York stone, reclaimed timber. They brought equipment – bulldozers, diggers, forklifts. They delivered workmen and craftsmen who were barracked in temporary accommodation built into the old stable block of Calve di Vazze – the island's lone but large residence. Fenster stood watching this activity, wearing a bright blue jumpsuit, its zip drawn down almost to his belly, revealing the fuzzy brown hair of his chest. David Spotpal stood next to him, squinting into the turbulent, rotor-churned air.

'We will build your castle, *Herr* Spotpal – we will create your principality – and it will be unlike any yet constructed.' Fenster clutched his copy of the blueprint in both hands. Spotpal said nothing. He merely watched the Sea Kings unloading their cargo and then rising into the air again, like giant wasps, armoured and prehistoric, hovering awkwardly in the Mediterranean light.

The work went slowly at first. The weather that year was unusually stormy. There were times when Lalouppe became covered in a permanent mist – the ocean atomised into billions of microscopic droplets that bound together to create a dense cloud. Some of the men rebelled – they objected to the Spartan conditions and Fenster's exacting standards. If details were not executed perfectly – to the millimetre – then work was torn down, broken up and begun again. But gradually, as the nights lengthened, Fenster's vision began to emerge from the crags and cliffs, growing like black crystals against the azure sky. A second wave of contractors arrived, replacing the first. They were more refined in manner – specialists, craftsmen, technicians, gathered from all around the world. Blacksmiths from Poland, clockmakers from Switzerland, computer engineers from the San Fernando Valley, each came in to play his part at the appointed time. A year after they had stood together facing into the ocean wind, Spotpal found himself next to Fenster, staring at a transformed topography. Lalouppe had been remade in Spotpal's image.

'Were you back in your *mutter*'s womb – you could not feel safer,' said the architect pressing his foot down lightly on one of the sensitised slabs of York stone. 'It has been the dream of man since he first crept into a cave to know such security. Come – I will show you . . .'

The interior of Calve di Vazze had not been radically altered, at least not in any way that was apparent to the casual observer. It had been tastefully renovated certainly – wallpaper from de Gournay, polished maple wood floors, Ambaji marble in the bathroom. But the spirit and feel of the house were not dissimilar to when Spotpal had first walked in there nearly three years earlier. This was not true of what lay beneath the building's surfaces. Every centimetre had been completely rewired, replumbed and reserviced. And deep within the house – or more accurately below it, since Fenster had tunnelled down some distance under the original cellars – there beat an entirely new heart of his creation.

They were standing before a bookshelf in a nondescript corridor behind the kitchen.

'You will see,' said Fenster, adjusting the tilt of his three-cornered Napolean hat, 'that there is a copy of the *London A–Z* on the shelves.' Spotpal nodded. 'Partly to remind you of your humble roots of course, but it serves a dual purpose.' The architect reached up and gently pushed the book's spine. The bookcase swung to one side with alarming speed, revealing a dark stairwell beyond.

They walked for some time, or so it felt to Spotpal. They must have been twenty metres below the rest of the house. Although the stairs had been plain concrete, the room they reached was itself lined with polished oak and equipped with a three-seater La Corbusier sofa. The only other furniture was a slim computer monitor and keyboard on a low wooden table, comfortably within reach of the sofa itself.

'Look closely, *Herr* Spotpal, and I will walk you through every facility of your new abode. It is quite unlike anything

conceived by any other mind. I believe the Pharaohs themselves would have been proud to reside here.' He switched
the computer screen on and for a moment it hummed white,
filling the dark room with its glare.

Later, after his initial tutorial, Spotpal walked with Fenster
around the island while the architect demonstrated in actuality what had merely been illustrated on the screen.

'There is not a centimetre of this island that is not wired or
monitored or known about by the system. Even the surrounding ocean is constantly watched by the radar – you are
alerted if any individual comes within three kilometres. It is
not possible for a person to be closer than that without you
knowing exactly where they are. And if you know exactly
where they are – you can deal with them.' Suddenly, theatrically, something sprung out of the ground. Spotpal was
disorientated for a moment. Polished steel bars surrounded
them, glinting in the sunlight. They were standing in a cage –
about three metres square – from which there was no possible
escape.

'It is concealed in the earth, *Herr* Spotpal, contained in its
own housing. The ceiling locks and assembles as it rises.
There is no way out – without the key.' The architect produced an anonymous-looking fob with a button on, which he
pressed. With the same startling speed the cage disassem-
bled itself and returned beneath the ground. The only
evidence of its presence was a faint, dark line around the
paving stones' edge from whence it sprang. 'Now this is all
powered by electricity and controlled by computer. Please,
be reassured that the back-up system is modelled on the
very same one utilised by the Airbus 330 – the safest
commercial airliner in existence.' Fenster looked around
himself into the empty air. 'This cage is but one of numer-
ous such devices spaced regularly around your island, *mein
Herr* – all of which you can control from any point in the
house. You will see the monitoring system gives you a thousand eyes in the night – like a spider in the middle of her

web. Should – by some impossible set of circumstances – a trespasser stray on to your domain, well—', Spotpal smiled to himself, 'you would be as a god to them. A cruel and capricious god if you so chose who could toy with the intruder as a cat toys with a sparrow.' The two men walked on along the scrubby ground. The temperature had risen, an oily haze smeared itself across the horizon. 'Of course the surest system must always have a contingency. An airline pilot who has lost all power knows he still has a chance of gliding his plane down to the earth. If – by some dark miracle – your power was to fail and your back-up was to fail and the back-up of your back-up was to fail, would you then become suddenly exposed? Is it possible for the hunter in his lair to become the prey?' Fenster had leaped out in front of Spotpal, adopting a ludicrously pantomimic pose. Spotpal regarded him with an expression somewhere between mild puzzlement and irritation. 'The answer of course is no. For we had discussed the concept of total security and total security was the brief. Total security is what you have, *Herr* Spotpal. As no one has had it before.' Fenster clapped his hands. 'Come – I will explain . . .'

They made their way back to the house, along the plain, stone causeway that led to the front entrance.

'Electronics of course can fail. Computer systems can fail. These things are possible. Mechanical devices are surer. These rely on the laws of physics – and the laws of physics, they never fail. It is not *möglich*. The house itself has a mechanical system that will turn it into a trap. And so we may be sure – you may be sure – of your ultimate safety – I have made that trap a lethal one. In the last instance Death sits between you and your pursuers – as implacable and inevitable as the setting sun. Let me demonstrate.'

They passed inside and mounted the stairs, climbing to the master bedroom. Fenster talked as they walked. 'The mechanism can be set in motion from any room in the house. Each has a similar system installed – there is no way of overriding it. You only have to ensure that you have the instantiation process retained in your memory – and you are safe. The system itself functions as a giant clock. It needs winding – but this process is mostly automatic. A physical intervention – a maintenance service – is required but once a year. I will supervise it myself.' He smiled, and his cater-pillar moustache expanded, like a furry concertina.

The following evening, the first night Spotpal was to spend alone on Lalouppe, he sat on the terrace in an Arne Jacobson chair and watched the last helicopter ascend into the amber sky. He listened to its roar diminish into a buzz and then almost to nothing – a tiny particle of sound among an infinity of others: the timpani of the ocean against the rocks, the insects chirruping in the long grass, the ice crack-ing in his glass of Belgian beer. He let the sense of being alone settle over him. He began to feel something – some-thing familiar but not experienced for decades – a waft of his earliest memories. Perhaps it was peace. The feeling lingered for a moment like a mist above the sea. Then his imagination attempted to destroy it. An image of a boat creeping up on the far side of the island – frogmen with rope-ladders and grappling irons, free to take Spotpal apart at their leisure, for no one would ever hear his screams or be aware of his suffer-ing. But then he withdrew the mini-laptop from his pocket and logged into the system. Typing in his password he accessed the main security menu, clicked on the camera icon and the sonar scans. Immediately a number of displays appeared chained across the screen. One displayed a slideshow of the island's perimeter. With surprising clarity each frame revealed nothing but waves crashing against unscalable rocks. The radar showed no vessels anywhere within its purview. The grid-pressure sensor system revealed nothing moving anywhere on the island. Spotpal studied these various readouts over the next few hours – as the sun descended beneath the rock-strewn horizon. He was amazed at the sense of connection they gave him with the place, as if

Lalouppe was now an extension of his consciousness – part of his nervous system. Fenster's design was brilliant indeed. This was no mere burglar alarm – the interface had been crafted with intelligence and sensitivity, creating an intuitive sense of oneness with the whole environment; of knowing everything one could know about it at any given moment. Spotpal might never have been able to articulate this, but in fact it was exactly what he had always craved. With a rising sense of excitement he realised that Fenster's system was answering the need in him that he had always thought could never be answered.

He jumped to his feet, holding the mini-laptop balanced on his left palm, and grabbed the cushion he had been leaning on. Pausing to click on a particular function on the security screen, he set off to the east of the house, in the direction of the bay – Lalouppe's only feasible access point. Lights mounted in trees and occasionally on poles flicked on as he walked past, illuminating the path he chose, like some hero in a Norse legend. When he had reached a spot halfway between the house and the island's edge he threw the cushion as hard as he could without aiming it in any specific direction. It landed about fifteen metres from where he stood, behind a patch of scrubby gorse. He squatted down on the floor, searching for a particular icon on the computer's desktop. He clicked on it and selected the function he required from the menu. Instantly one of Fenster's huge cages flew from the ground, clicking into place, somewhat absurdly around it – a Dali painting brought to life: cage with cushion in a moonlit landscape. Spotpal walked towards it, pressing his head against the bars. He looked down at the piece of soft furnishing now imprisoned until he chose to release it. He laughed. He laughed and he laughed and he laughed. And then he took himself to bed and he slept with a consistency and a depth he had no memory of ever achieving in his adult life.

And this sensation persisted – over the coming nights –

weeks of them – whenever Spotpal's treacherous imagination produced a 'but', he was able to counter it with some element of Fenster's system. However devious the portion of his brain that devised these torments was, it was outwitted by Fenster, who had been even more so. You think someone may be tunnelling up through the cliffs? Not possible – check this readout of seismic activity sensitive enough to pick up the vibrations of a dentist's drill. You think someone's flying overhead? The separate earth to air radar system would have picked up the intrusion and alerted you of it some time before the thought occurred to you. And even had you detected an unwanted visitor – well, retreat to the house, flip the secure switch, let the shutters come down and toy with them until they leave. What Fenster had done was give Spotpal a kit of tools which could be applied effectively to every scenario he could conjure. Together they formed a key, one that unlocked a door to a particular kind of freedom Spotpal had never known – the freedom that came with peace. It was not the countering of the imaginings themselves that did this – it was the fact that over time, and not that long a time, Spotpal's mind began to tire of the game of devising them only to have them so effectively neutralised on each occasion. And thus finally – after decades of ingenuity – his tormented fictions subsided.

And Spotpal began a new life. Solitariness had become so ingrained in him that he did not baulk at it. It was not why he had chosen this existence but it was a not unwelcome by-product. His internet connection opened the whole world to him. He began many online relationships – at first observing others at a distance through the pages of Facebook and MySpace, and then gradually making associations with some personalities who appealed. He would play the markets too, not because he needed to add to his wealth, though the purchase and development of Lalouppe had made a sizeable dint in it. Rather Spotpal enjoyed the sense of connection that accompanied the activity – observing the actions and reactions of others as it impacted on the price of shares and the rate of trade. And so his life continued for some months – untroubled by any of the darker aspects beyond the foam-dashed fringes of the island. Food was delivered from the mainland every twelve weeks or so. He began to cultivate a small vegetable plot, and to tend the orchard and vinery to the rear of the house. Though Spotpal had no experience with horticulture his attention was enough to bring the old trees back into some semblance of health and as September approached he was able to enjoy the pleasure of eating grapes directly from the branch.

This idyll may have persisted for the rest of Spotpal's days had chance not intervened. But intervene it did and in the mundane form of a Sunday magazine article. An in-depth career retrospective of Franz Fenster, in the form of an inter-view and pull-out wallchart, was the fuse for what followed. Fenster had assured Spotpal he was as discreet as a royal gynaecologist yet he could not help but allude, when probed, to some of the revolutionary aspects of his commission, par-ticularly those relating to the idea of absolute security. And those allusions were enough to bait the interest of Aslo Kastriot, who read the article on a flight from Heathrow to Zagreb on the day of its publication.

And who was Aslo Kastriot? His name was unknown to even the most informed of European police chiefs but he was in fact the force behind the force – the power behind the power – of nearly four hundred criminal gangs that operated from St Petersburg in the east to Belfast in the west. Nine words in the article were enough to excite Kastriot's interest: 'a place of unassailable and absolute security and privacy'. For like David Spotpal, Aslo Kastriot had a vision. His vision was about freedom too – the freedom to express his will, unbound by the law, or any notion of the law. Of course had it occurred to Kastriot, he could have found his own island, commissioned Franz Fenster to build his own version of Lalouppe and Calve di Vazze. He certainly had the resources to bring such a project into being. He stretched out in his seat, holding the olive from his Martini loosely in his hand. The plane banked to the right, turning away from the ground and forcing him into the sky, the weight of the earth pulling against him. The olive rolled in Kastriot's fist and he closed it, holding the wet fruit tightly. Why build, when you can take, he thought.

It was a simple matter to get to Fenster. The man was a fool who had no idea of the world and the state of potential threat that he – and everybody else – was under every second of their life. When Fenster came home that day to his Ringstrasse apartment he was actually smiling – smiling to himself though no one else was present. Kastriot, who was sitting cross-legged on the floor waiting for him, was fascinated to see that the smile remained frozen on Fenster's face for a good five seconds after Kastriot shot the man's shin out with his Beretta.

'Good afternoon, *Herr* Fenster.'

The architect was gulping now, trying to take in enough air to keep pace with his accelerating heart. He had yet to cry out. The pain would not hit for another thirty seconds or more, depending on his metabolic rate.

David Spotpal was waiting. Waiting for his first visitor from the world beyond his realm. There had been four deliveries of provisions since he had been there. The supply drop was organised by his agents on the mainland – who were in fact Swiss rather than Corsican. He preferred the neutrality of this arrangement – there was less opportunity for it to be corrupted by some outside influence. But Spotpal had not been in the presence of another human being since Fenster had departed and he had watched the architect's helicopter fading into the ocean mist. And now Fenster was to be his first guest, together with a small team of technicians. This fact didn't trouble Spotpal. If he so chose he could ask his agents to arrange for other company. But he did not choose. After the first two months had passed he had decided the isolation he was experiencing was the best friend he had ever had. And here was the helicopter, tiny at first, the dull throb of its blades carried ahead by the wind. Spotpal stood, a hundred metres from the cliff edge watching it approach.

He thought for a moment how best to greet the architect. Always self-conscious at such times, Spotpal began to feel himself tighten up. And yet he wanted Fenster to know how much he was enjoying living on Lalouppe and benefiting from the fruits of the architect's efforts. The helicopter descended with unexpected speed. It was a large yellow Bell 24. Not as sizeable as the Sea Kings that had been used in the construction period, but big enough to carry a number of crew. Fenster had originally told Spotpal that the servicing was deliberately designed to be a simple matter and that different aspects of the system would be attended to at different times. Consequently he would never need to bring more than two technicians at a time – and the work could be carried out within an eighteen-hour period so there would never be any need for anyone to stay overnight.

Was Spotpal alarmed when he saw four figures climbing out of the helicopter and jumping down on to the gravelly ground of Lalouppe's high plateau? Well, yes he was. Six months or more of respite from his demons had not erased the tramlines carved in his consciousness over the preceding years. And within an instant of seeing Fenster, hobbling towards him across the concourse, Spotpal's thoughts began racing along those familiar pathways. It wasn't Fenster's injured appearance alone that set off Spotpal's fears, it was the contrast with the three grey-bodysuited accomplices – their faces covered by white masks and goggles. Fenster – whose lower leg was encased in a cast – was walking at the head of this group, but he did not have the look of the man with authority over others whom Spotpal remembered. And then, almost as quickly as his habitual fears had re-established themselves, Spotpal realised that in this domain he himself was in charge. He reached in his back pocket for the mini-laptop –

the one he kept with him at all times. He accessed the security menu and enabled the cage setting. Within a few seconds the visitors found themselves surrounded by a titanium enclosure. One of the suited figures' feet had become caught in the metal as it rose from the ground. He was pulled up for a few moments, launched into the air at speed. He lifted himself up against the bars, freeing his leg from them with twisting athleticism before falling to the ground, seemingly uninjured. If everything was bona fide Spotpal could apologise – but a rule he had learned early in business and one he carried over to his private life was 'never apologise and never explain'.

Of the many things that Spotpal could have done – not that he would have known this of course – erecting an impenetrable cage between himself and Kastriot was the most egregious. For two years, between the ages of five and seven, the Albanian's stepfather kept him in a cage. It had begun as a game. Treat the boy like a dog. He had to lap water from a steel bowl. If he picked it up Kastriot's fingers were rapped with a rusty pipe that his stepfather kept close like a cane. Kastriot would then drop the bowl of water, soaking his bare torso, and there would be no more until the next day. This game quickly ceased being a game and established itself as a norm. His mother said nothing. He was kept in such a state of starvation that when the old man threw scraps through the bars of the cage – which had been built to keep chickens – Kastriot would scrabble around the floor locating whatever they were with his mouth, swallowing them whole because he was too hungry to be able to bear the wait of chewing. This situation may have continued into puberty had his stepfather not been killed in a brawl. That night, without a word being spoken, his mother undid the cage's heavy padlock. Nothing more was ever said. Three weeks later Kastriot found his stepfather's grave and dug up the corpse on his own. He set about it, kicking it, punching it, stamping on the head until he wept. But the pain and rage he felt were only intensified for there was no relief or satisfaction in the act, his stepfather's rotting body a limp carcass beneath him.

And so – now he found himself in another cage, on a strange island, and for a moment, less than a second, he was back there submerged in the unspeakable pain of his memory. He struck out, kicking Fenster's injured leg with such force that the plaster cast shattered. The architect's howl echoed off the distant walls of Calve di Vazze. Seeing this – and worse, hearing it – made Spotpal turn around and run back towards the house, experiencing an adrenal dump he had not felt since his own childhood. Kastriot unzipped his bodysuit and withdrew his Beretta – he aimed it at Spotpal and fired off three shots. They all missed.

'Remove this or you will know more pain than you will be able to bear,' Kastriot said to Fenster – regaining control of himself. Fenster, who was leaning against the bars of the cage, his eyes closed, emitted a whimper. He reached into his pocket and withdrew the controlling key fob he had retained. He prayed – not that he was a believing man – that Spotpal had not reset the security protocols since he had demonstrated them. But Spotpal hadn't – there was no reason he would have done – and the cage unmade itself, sliding back into its hidden housing with an elegance and grace which impressed the part of Fenster that even in these extremes discerned such aesthetics.

Spotpal was nearly at the house. His chest hurt. He had a stitch. He had not run like this since his schooldays. His mind churned. Was this a nightmare? Such a thing could not be happening. He wanted to experience the relief that came with the customary realisation that his fear was imagined. He risked a glance over his shoulder. The cage had gone. He tried to assess what was taking place though his terror made it difficult. Who were these men? They were with Fenster. That was Fenster with them, wasn't it? How else could the cage have been disabled. This was Spotpal's mistake. This was the one desperate flaw in his system of perfect security that even his normally ferocious imagination had failed to perceive: what if Fenster went bad? What if Fenster was the one? He tried to think as he ran. Tried to let his instincts take over. Something hot flew past his ear – a bee on fire. Then, a slice of a second behind it, a sharp sound somewhere between a crack and a pop. He was being shot at. The hair above his temple was lifted by an incendiary tube of air. Another report behind. He had to get in the house. He didn't think it was possible to run faster than he had been but the adrenaline pushed his legs beyond the limits of anything they had experienced. For the first time in Spotpal's life his fight or flight reflex was functioning appropriately. His mind became clear, his focus absolute. He remembered Fenster's words. The architect was with him at his side, taking the slow walk through Calve di Vazze: 'The mechanism can be set in motion from any room in the house. Each has a similar system installed – there is no way of overriding it. You only have to ensure that you have the instantiation process retained in your memory – and you are safe.' He was inside now. The cool air of the old mansion surrounded him. He did not want to look over his shoulder to see how long he had. They must still be a hundred metres or so behind him. He could visualise the red button and the smaller black button above it, behind the wheeled cocktail cabinet. He flung the piece of furniture aside. 'There is no way of overriding this system.' Those were the architect's words. Were they true? Let them be true.

Bless Fenster for his curious wit – regardless of his treachery, for there was no way of forgetting the mnemonic he had assigned to the sequences of button-pushes required to initialise the mechanical system. One on the red, two on the black, one on the red, one on the black, two on the red – 'shave and a haircut, two bits'. It was done. A slow grumble began below Spotpal, under the maple wood floor, like some monstrous central heating system coming on. A series of distant jerks and judders echoed and grew, unfurling beneath him. But the intruders were visible through the window. The tallest of them. The one with the gun. He was nearly at the edge of the lawn. Thwwwwwtttt. The window was no more. It had been replaced by black anodised steel. It lined the entirety of the outside wall. No one was coming in the house. And Spotpal was not going out. He lay there on the wood floor, his heart clapping in his chest, his breath beyond control. He panicked that he might pass out. He didn't. Gradually his heart-rate slowed. He was able to breathe. He was able to think. Would the second aspect of Fenster's system work? Sitting up on his elbows he reached for the laptop in his back pocket. Now all he could do was tune in to the cameras at the front of the house and watch.

Kastriot and his men had come to a rest, panting like a football team at half-time. Fenster limped behind them, unsure where to go or what to do. He stopped and sat on the floor – an injured animal, all hope gone, meekly accepting of whatever was to follow. He stared up at the black steel and the breathless white-suited men in front of it.

'What is this?' said Kastriot. 'You did not speak of this.' Exhausted by his own fear, too exhausted to feel it, Fenster leaned back on the grass.

'Fail-safe,' he said. The words hung there without further qualification. Kastriot stared down at him. Eventually he responded.

'Make it go up. Now.'

Fenster looked up at the Albanian. He shook his head.

'You're not saying no to me, *Herr* Fenster. No one says no to me.'

Fenster shrugged. 'Can't be done.'

'You didn't speak of this,' said Kastriot again.

Another pause. Then Fenster said, 'I didn't think it would get this far. He – Spotpal – would get this far.'

'Well, he did.' Kastriot looked down at the architect, refusing to let the man free from his gaze.

'We can break through.'

'How?'

'With oxyacetylene.'

'He will be contacting the outside world. Will he not? As we speak.'

'That can be stopped.' Fenster waved his laptop.

Kastriot maintained his gaze. 'There are many ways to die *Herr* Fenster – as you know. I have seen most of them. Observed their effect. A man can die welcoming death. It has its own momentum. It can be a friend. And a man can die hating it – feeling every fading heartbeat as fear, as rage, as unspeakable suffering. A man can be made to die that way. The natural processes which are there to comfort can be interrupted. Perverted. There are technologies for doing so – techniques. I know most of them. I've studied them.' He nodded slightly, then turned to face his subordinates. 'To the helicopter. The gas-axe,' he said.

'Is there anything we need to know,' said Kastriot as his team prepared the oxyacetylene torch, igniting the gas and burning off a few experimental bursts of laser-blue flame. 'Think carefully before you answer.' Fenster was lying out on the grass in front of the house, looking as relaxed as if he were on a family picnic. His own mini-laptop, which replicated the one Spotpal used to access Lalouppe's system, was open in front of him.

'He will be inside, close to the front door. I have disabled the visual and radar-based surveillance systems.' Fenster swivelled the screen round, offering it to Kastriot in support of his statement. Kastriot let his eyes rest on the display for a few moments then returned his gaze to the injured architect. He said nothing. Fenster filled the silence. 'He will be inside to the left of the front door. There is a mechanical viewing device – a periscope of sorts. I can guarantee it.'

Kastriot reached for his Beretta. He wanted the certainty of turning Spotpal off himself. He continued studying Fenster, however. It was no good incapacitating the architect further – he was the only possible means available of controlling this most hostile of environments. But the man was just about smart enough to know this himself. Here was a delicate chess game. Everything was a chess game, but the heightened nature of these circumstances made Kastriot's favoured metaphor even more illuminating than usual. Keeping his face impassive he imagined himself as the architect, conjuring the man's fear and pain within. He sensed the advantage – knowing all the workings of this most secure and lethal of places. If he were Fenster he would want one thing more than any other. He would want Kastriot dead. Kastriot was the source of his suffering and his predicament. If Kastriot ended he took all that with him. The others could be dealt with easily. Fenster would know where to go, what to do. He was only a short step from being safe. The means for Kastriot's demise were all around him – accessible through the computer.

'You will give this to me,' said Kastriot, speaking almost as the thought hit him. 'You will give this to me and walk with me.' The Albanian's brain continued calculating. If Fenster knew that Kastriot wouldn't risk him dead this might cushion him from fear. The man must be kept frightened. Moving suddenly Kastriot grabbed the man's hand, held the muzzle of the gun to his middle finger and squeezed the trigger. The member exploded in a red cloud of flesh and cordite. Fenster howled in shock. He bent over and began to retch. Kastriot pulled him upright, dragging him towards the oxyacetylene torch. He clicked his fingers and one of his men handed him the blue-burning nozzle. Kastriot aimed it at Fenster's injury, cauterising the wound. The architect's scream hurt his ears. Kastriot pulled him close.

'I am inside your head, *Herr* Fenster. I know what you are planning. It is not going to come about. You understand me. There is much that can be done to you that will not kill you. Consider your advice carefully.' Fenster moaned. He collapsed on to his knees. He would not speak. With a simple movement of his head Kastriot sent two of his men to the steel-covered front door.

Without caution, with purpose, they marched towards the black-lidded face of the house. The taller of the two lay down the equipment and began to approach the area of steel covering the door, with the apparent aim of examining it. Suddenly and without any prelude he was thrown high into the air. Some chrome device had sprung from the ground under him, like the blades of a giant pair of scissors. The man's grey-booted feet were caught in hoops at their ends. As the metal prongs flew upwards they parted at great speed. There was a terrible rending sound, like heavy fabric being ripped, accompanied by a brief yell. Then, abruptly, there were two men flying through the air. But it wasn't two men. It was the same man divided. He flew away from himself – split laterally – one half flung east, the other west. Blood dropped from the sky like a biblical curse. It landed pattering on to stone. The other man, who had been standing closer to the equipment, took a step backwards, his neck craned, head towards the clouds, following the twin trajectories of his colleague. And then he was no more. A great slab of York stone on some kind of pivot sprang upwards out of the ground and fell back flattening him with enormous force. More blood pooled out across the patio. An amount of it was splattered upwards in a great arc, vivid against the black steel of the security panels. The tank of the oxyacetylene burner rolled back slightly, disturbed by the abrupt motion of this action, coming to a rest a few inches from where it had been lain.

Kastriot remained motionless, observing this carnage. He stood, absorbing it, his head ranging slightly from left to right in order to take it in. Then he turned to face Fenster. But Fenster was already crawling away from him, towards the torture garden revealed in the stone-slabbed area at the front of the house.

'Fenster,' said Kastriot, calling out in a voice resonant with force and authority. The architect turned his head to face Kastriot, though he maintained his slow crawl across the stone. Kastriot recognised the look on Fenster's face. He didn't like it. It was the look of a man who had made a decision. 'Fenster. Stop.' Kastriot held up the gun. But Fenster kept crawling, aiming for some definite spot. Kastriot called out but before the sound had left his mouth Fenster was no more – sandwiched between two huge hunks of stone that had snapped upwards flattening him like a flower in a book.

The only smart thing to do was to leave. The terrain was too dangerous and it wasn't worth the cost. Kastriot was aware of this – he could sense it quite calmly within – but some other imperative had taken over. He was not going to be defeated by this worm who had caged him with such ease.

But what to do first? What was the strategy to be? There was always a strategy. Always a good choice and a bad choice, or if not a good choice a better and worse choice. The trick of it was to make a decision, to act, to avoid procrastination. Paradoxically, doing nothing could sometimes be that action. He stared at the house, at the ground which intervened between him and it, the slashes of blood, the offal-smeared stone. He tried to reduce the circumstances to a mathematical problem. In maths there was always a solution. One merely had to get to it. He breathed deeply. Exhaled, feeling the air cold against the insides of his nostrils. His goal? To get to the house, with the burner. Then he merely had to get inside. Everything after that was easy. It would not be hard to break the worm. He would fix on him, seek him, crack him. It was all a question of decision. The first thing was to think like Fenster, to be in his no-longer-existent head. There was distance between Kastriot and the house. There were potentially many more devices hidden that may yet burst into action if he were to trigger them. But there were restrictions on the possibilities for the laying of these traps. Simple things like surface area, the amount of mechanics the ground could contain, the space needed for those mechanics to work. Kastriot began to walk around the house. The paving surrounded it like a moat. Potentially every inch of it concealed death.

Spotpal observed this through his little periscope – his

pursuer prowling slowly and carefully, reduced to a beautifully clear and bright figurine by the Swiss optics Fenster had so fastidiously employed. Spotpal felt the sweat on his back and beneath his armpits. He knew he wasn't safe – not while that figurine was still moving. The man's purpose was apparent even in miniature. The safest action would be to retire to the subterranean control room. Gather all the provisions he could find, fill every jug, glass and bottle with water, and let it become a war of attrition. If he could take all food from the house he would have a much greater advantage – after all there was little else to eat to be found on Lalouppe. Or would Fenster have told the man about the control room's existence. Even with the secret door bolted from within the gas burner would ultimately prevail. If that was the case Calve di Vazze had become little more than a holding pen for Spotpal prior to his inevitable slaughter.

Kastriot looked up at the sky. It was beginning to darken, the clouds standing out in sharper relief against the reddening blue. He did not want to be out here in the darkness. The worm would have too much of the advantage. Kastriot could stay in the helicopter, but he could not risk it being damaged in any way. He did not want to have to deal with being stuck on this storm-blasted rock without possession of the house at its heart. He returned to his original position, in front of Calve di Vazze's main entrance. The Albanian sat on the cold grass, feeling its dampness through the cotton of his trousers. He looked at the chessboard in front of him. It was possible to work out where the mechanisms of the traps already sprung would be. Their motors were driven by potential energy – simple but powerful spring releases. Such machinery needed to be of a certain size and scale in order to function. Therefore if one took a path to the house that ran between these devices there was a reasonable likelihood that no other apparatus could be buried there. Admittedly the last six or seven metres were more dangerous but he would deal with them when he reached them.

The burner still lay where it had come to rest, its hose and nozzle coiled neatly at one end. It wasn't too far from the path Kastriot had drawn out in his head. If he made it to the house he would return along the safe route and get it. Better to explore the terrain unencumbered. He looked for something he could use to poke the ground ahead of him. There were few trees, at least on this side of the house, but a brief search yielded a piece of bamboo cane – the kind that might be used to cultivate tomato plants. When he picked the cane up there was a line of yellow grass beneath it, as if it had lain there unnoticed for some time. Holding it in front of him as he walked, Kastriot tapped it gently up and down, like a blind man.

The one outcome that Kastriot was not going to accept was his death. He had resisted it, not just as a reality, but as a possibility since he was seven years old, when he had first grasped the idea of what the word meant. Nothing would obliterate him. It was not going to happen. In adulthood, in his maturity, it was not a matter of fear. He feared nothing. He was master of everything he chose to be master of. There was an absolute block on the possibility. A slab of black granite he carried before him into the future.

He studied the earth in front of him, taking in every centimetre. The ground gave away very little information. Kastriot reached out with his will, used every aspect of his senses to determine what was there. Instinct was a powerful force, perhaps the most powerful of the many facilities he drew on. He prepared himself to move fast at the first suggestion of a tremor. Anything might give it away. A change in air pressure. A smell of axel grease as a mechanism was tripped. He risked a look up at the house. He had covered about a third of the distance he needed to. If he could just—. The ground fell away under him. He was falling before he realised what had happened. How far would he drop? He reached out with his hands, felt them flailing against earth. A heavy thump. The impact forced the air from his lungs. Whatever he had landed on was juddering beneath him, vibrating like the surface of a washing machine. Two pieces of heavy stone had dropped on either side of him trapping his arms before he could move them. He turned his head slowly to the left. He saw his forearm crushed beneath a dark mass. He pulled. The pain bit like an animal. Light began to fill the space around him. He was on some kind of platform. It was emerging from the hole he had fallen into, rising into the open air like a cinema organ. Something fell on his foot. He attempted to pull back the other, the left one. Torment was coming at him from all sides – from his shattered forearms, from his injured ankles. The hurt in his right foot had a different character – it was pulsating rhythmically, a regular speedy beat like a palpitating heart. The agony was gradually rising up his leg. The block of stone was pounding his limb relentlessly, like a pestle in a mortar. It was on some mechanism that made it bounce up and down, shifting inexorably towards him. He moved his other leg as fast as he could, as far as he could, but he was limited by his physiology. He tried to pull it up under his buttocks. The bouncing stone chewed its way up his body. He could only resist it with his mind. His body was already going. It was white. A whiteness consuming him. He refused to express it as a scream. He clenched his throat, his lungs, his stomach. The matter that was being taken away from him. He looked up. The sky was obscured. The man from the house was peering down at him.

David Spotpal looked down at his pursuer – face to face at last. The man – about his own age, his face contorted like a woman giving birth – looked up at him. There was a smell like wet iron, blood and urine mingling in a pool around what was left of the man's body. Spotpal found himself staring into a pair of dying eyes, life still apparent, holding on despite the pain. The only sound was the percussion of the machine bouncing and grinding. Spotpal felt no fear for himself any more, only an awareness of the fear in the already coffined person below him. The man was trying to speak. The oscillating, consuming block of stone was at the man's pelvis, shattering it into mulch inside him. Spotpal, to his own surprise, felt himself leaning closer. And another feeling overcame him. He wanted to help. He must return to the house and shut the mechanism down – or at least see if it was possible. He stood up and turned but the man tried to call out to him. Spotpal couldn't understand the words but the request in the cry was clear. 'Don't leave me.' Spotpal came back. The man was dying – perhaps about to pass in the next few seconds. The fingers of his left hand twitched, jutting from beneath their imprisoning stone. Spotpal reached for them. The man tried to hold on, a delicate touch almost like a child's. He released the scream he had been retaining. His fingers attempted to tighten. Spotpal tightened his own grip. He looked for something in the other man's face but everything was gone. He squeezed hard, as if this might bring the man back to him. The wind picked up around him, the air contracting above the cooling ocean. It was too late. He stared down at the mess of pulp and matter.

He felt the responsibility for the pain in which the man had died pressing on him, closing round him like a cage.

He filled his lungs with air.

He screamed into the unperceiving wind.

David Spotpal left Lalouppe that December. He buried what he could find of the bodies, deep in the orchard, beneath the newly fruiting apple trees. The helicopter he dismantled. It became a project. Each component he removed was tossed into the churning sea. Pieces that were too large to move he broke down into manageable units with the oxyacetylene torch. Eventually that too was claimed by the ocean. It was time to return to the mainland.

Sitting in his chartered Sea King, the wet tiled roof of Calve di Vazze shining in the winter sun, receding below, Spotpal reflected on an idea that was new to him, which had recently found purchase in his mind: there were many things to fear in life but death wasn't one of them. Dying alone, however – that was a different matter.

Yani's Day

How many years is it now since Yani began his long walk? Twenty? Twenty-five? I, as I'm sure do you, remember only too vividly how it began.

The reports of the deaths came first. They started in the North-West. A farmer, an elderly walker, a middle-aged woman. All with advanced cancer. Naturally the papers seized upon the fact that not one of them had been previously diagnosed with the disease. In fact, according to her GP, the middle-aged woman had undergone a routine examination the week before and had not shown a single symptom. The corpses were found about half a mile from each other in open countryside near Bolton Abbey. And the story ignited upon the discovery of the next four bodies, between Sedburgh and Burnside. This time two children were among them – a brother and sister aged nine and thirteen. Again the cause of death in all cases was cancer in its most extreme stages, and again in all but one of the cases there had been no history of symptoms or any medical presentation whatsoever. A multitude of theories about the possible causes flooded the media: the volume of wireless networks, mobile phone masts, large concentrations of a particular species of bracken. It was several days before a journalist made the geographical connection – the bodies were all laid out in regular intervals along the Pennine Way.

When the deaths ceased for a number of days there was a state of national relief. Perhaps understandably something about these reports had insinuated itself into the collective psyche and contributed to a growing sense of unease. And then another victim was found. This time near East Ilsley. And more sinisterly this man wasn't quite dead. He was struggling to breathe when he was found and was able to stay alive long enough to describe what had happened. He was – or had been – in good health. A regular rambler familiar with long walks and the vicissitudes that accompanied them, he had never had a day of ill health in his life. And yet this agonising fate had befallen him during a relaxed stroll along the Ridgeway. He had been crossing a stile and had paused to allow a large man in a distinctive floral shirt to pass. A few moments later he collapsed with an unbearable pain in the centre of his spine, which spread into his chest and ears. Mercifully, the walker died a short time after he gave his account. But when two more bodies were found – one near South Stoke and one near Goring – it was clear that there was to be no reprieve from this nightmare phenomenon. And another troubling detail emerged, one that was hard for the news media to make any sense of: the same oversized figure in the floral shirt had been seen near the third body, that of an elderly woman who had been out walking her dachshund. And another party reported that he had seen this floral-shirted figure crook his finger at the woman in a peculiar manner, just before she had collapsed.

Understandably perhaps, the press grasped these incidents and began to cook fantastic and sensational stories. The tabloids were the first to decide that the man in the floral shirt was central to what was occurring. Who was this mysterious figure? Could he destroy a person with a mere crook of a digit? Of course the broadsheets derived as much material from decrying the sensational and irresponsible speculation of the popular press. No one in those distant days would have considered that it was in fact the popular press which had been closest to the truth.

The matter was settled by some mobile-phone video

footage shot by a teenage girl near Pangbourne. She had seen the man in the floral shirt, recognised him from descriptions she had heard on television and immediately begun to record what she saw. First, however, she had concealed herself behind some trees, as quite understandably she wanted to avoid putting herself in any danger. Consequently the footage that was played over and over again in the succeeding days had the shaky and obscured quality of a Big-Foot sighting. A lumbering, hefty shape in an oddly bright shirt disappearing in and out of narrow trees. The shocking thing, the truly shocking thing, was seeing the figure raise its hand and watch a nearby child fall almost simultaneously, like a marionette suddenly deprived of its strings.

And then a new game began. 'Find the man in the floral shirt.' Inevitably there were sightings everywhere. Town centres, airports, motorway service stations. Each of them proved to be inaccurate. Innocent parties were harassed in their homes. And most notably the public footpaths of the various national trails emptied. The public had reached the conclusion that they were unsafe long before any government body issued an official warning. It was this fact presumably that precipitated the next sighting. Now that the national trails were unwalked, anyone using them became more obvious. And given that several national newspapers, not to mention a number of local ones, had taken to hiring helicopters and flying the length of the pathways in question to see if the figure was out there, it was only a matter of time before he was located. His vividly patterned attire was only too visible from any distance. He wore no coat. The news footage from that time still burns: Yani striding along with purpose – like some antediluvian animal on an atavistic course dictated by forces beyond its conscious control.

The police were waiting for him at Windsor. Of course they had nothing to charge him with. Their excuse was that it was for his own protection. But Yani did not stop walking.

He pushed through the lines of constables awaiting him as if they were shoppers on Oxford Street, unconnected with him and the imperative of his mission. He ignored all attempts to speak to him, made by those who ran after him. Some cars drove on to the next convenient stopping point. The intervention was going to become, by necessity, more aggressive. Yani had been asked to halt by a number of uniformed police officers and he had refused, oblivious to their authority. The police had no choice but to apprehend him. Once again Yani ignored them, and so two officers were dispatched to bring him to a halt by physical means. Yani did not even look back as they approached. He merely held up his hand and crooked his right index finger. Both officers collapsed writhing to the floor.

This was the action, observed by the unwavering glare of the national media, that changed everything. This was the moment that redefined the world and our understanding of it. This was the point in history from which there was no return.

Everyone present had run to the assistance of the policemen. There was no surprise in the fact that Yani continued unhindered on his way.

The deaths of these two serving officers were unfortunately not isolated. While Yani's random killings seemed to have abated, at least as long as the footpaths remained clear, the death rate continued to rise. Anyone who approached him with malign intent was deprived of their life in the same unfussy manner. Vigilantes, local hardmen, ex-serving officers – all suffered the same excruciating end. And it seems that all those who bore Yani any ill will – or at least the intention to convert that ill will into action – were vulnerable. They did not even need to be in direct physical proximity to him. An SAS sniper was sent by high authority to end Yani's life. He had not even loaded his rifle when his body was found, some half a mile from Yani's dreadful course.

All we could do was observe. And Yani was observed. He didn't seem to need food, or even water, at least not on a regular basis. He was seen to sip intermittently from a cycler's canister that he kept in his small knapsack, slung most of the time over one shoulder. His pace rarely altered – a steady stride, which remained generally unaffected by the terrain. Physically it was hard to tell too much about him from a distance. But image enhancement revealed him to be middle-aged, maybe in his early forties, somewhat over-weight, with a light-coloured scrubby beard and similarly coloured lank hair. He didn't smile. He bore an expression of intense purpose, his eyes focused unfailingly on what lay immediately ahead of him and nothing further. Within less than a day of these images being published Yani was identi-fied. His name was Yani Raoul. He was forty-seven years old. He was a UK national by birth but his family was of North-African origin – though there must have been intermarriage because Yani looked almost entirely Caucasian. One photo-graph from his earlier life was to become as emblematic as Myra Hindley's headshot, or Peter Sutcliffe in his wedding suit. It was an image on an ID card from Yani's place of work – which was, of course, where I knew him from.

Yani was, or had been, a bookseller in Crewe, and prior to that had worked at Waterstone's on Charing Cross Road – a branch that no longer exists. Some two weeks before his first killing he had failed to show up for his shift one morning. This in itself was not unusual, though it was for Yani – he was known for his surly diligence. But after the seventh day of absence, and failing to get an answer from his contact address, numbers and email, the police were routinely informed. A week later Yani was on the Pennine Way. What had happened to make this gruff, isolated but by all accounts ultimately gentle individual into a murderous super-being, no one could say. Given the unprecedented nature of what was occurring, the authorities decided that Yani had to be interviewed. He had to tell his own story. Already – with fewer than six weeks having elapsed since the affair had begun – Yani was being perceived as a god in some quarters. And by some others as

God Himself. How else could our culture account for what was taking place? Certainly there were some, mostly risible, attempts by the materialists to cling on to the last shreds of their rationalism – talk of string theory, the anthropocentric universe and the theoretical ability of mind to bend what was around it. But we all knew it was guff. Ultimately most people fell back on a sort of 'there are more things on heaven and earth' philosophy and let the whole thing be. What they wanted to happen was for life to continue as it had done before. They tried. But it couldn't.

There were no deaths for a number of days. Yani strode on to the end of the Thames Path. And then, if it were possible, something even more disconcerting happened. Yani disappeared.

It didn't happen like a magic trick in a cloud of smoke, or even with the sudden pop of a special effect. He just seemed to be obscured by some trees from which he didn't emerge. After a certain length of time someone approached, very gently. There was no evidence of Yani at all.

Around an hour later he was sighted again. On the Cleveland Way almost three hundred miles to the north. Even in a helicopter the distance could not have been covered in that time. Why this should have been more disturbing than Yani's ability to end life with a casual movement of his hand it's hard to explain – unless it was the fact that he was now officially uncontainable. Maybe while he was still subject to the laws of physics there was comfort in the thought that someone, somewhere, would devise a way of stopping him – giving their own life to drive a lorry into him, or drop a weight on him from above from a remotely piloted plane – something – anything. But now. Now Yani could go from one place to another with no restriction. Now he seemed both supernaturally lethal and absolutely indestructible. The panic began. And it spread throughout the globe. Up until this point the Yani story had, perhaps surprisingly, been of only mild interest to the rest of the world – in the way we might only have had mild interest in claims of stigmata from India. But Yani's documented ability to transport himself at will from one place to another changed that. Now the world's press arrived to follow his progress.

And Yani's effect on the British population had become tangibly corrosive. A number of large churches were set on fire, including Southwark Cathedral. There was city-centre rioting and looting – not directly related to Yani's presence it's true, but fuelled by a growing sense that things were coming apart. Unspoken assumptions that had glued our secular society together had been shattered in a day, in a moment. People were blinking frightened in the glare of a new universe. There was only one option for the government. Someone had to talk to Yani, someone without a harmful thought in his head. Ironically, or perhaps not, a cleric was chosen. An unassuming moderate Sufi cleric called Kabir Emre. His brief was open – to begin a dialogue. His only instruction – to approach without a harmful thought in his mind. He took a gift of his own choosing – a perfectly ripe peach – but he carried nothing else when he was delivered to Llanbrynmair on the Glyndwr's Way. The cameras were held back. Police helicopters patrolled the skies to ensure that there was privacy from above too. It was reported that Yani did not pause when Emre approached, but neither did he resist being joined in any discernible way.

They talked for some considerable time though apparently they passed the first hour in silence. The peach was handed over. Yani expressed gratitude. And the parley began. Yani had only been waiting for this. He had wanted to talk from the beginning. Emre did not question, he listened. Yani knew the strength of his position – though he did not speak of how he had developed the powers he had been so brutally exercising. But his demands were simple. He had given much thought to them and they only consisted of this: he wanted to be in charge of his place of work – not the branch – but the whole chain. He wanted to become the CEO. He wanted to run the company. If this request were granted he would restrict any future killing to members of his staff.

Once Yani's desire was known I don't imagine there was any doubt that it would be granted. There was an amount of cosmetic procrastination, but not for very long. What Yani asked for – he got. Waterstone's was effectively nationalised and control handed to Yani. From that point on it became clear that – whatever might be stated publicly – the selling of books, the dissemination of literature, was removed from all obligations of the market. Yani could prove to be the worst CEO the company had ever been encumbered with and the government would still pour taxpayers' money into the organ-isation just to keep it afloat. In cash terms – as a percentage of GDP – the amounts would be relatively insignificant, so even on a cost-benefit analysis – mass death versus a nationalised booksellers – there was no debate to be had.

And this was how bookselling became simultaneously the highest-risk and the highest-paid retail occupation in exis-tence. In order to retain and to attract staff – who now had a statistically significant chance of dying in agony while under-taking their duties – wages had to shoot up. They had to, because without staff the shops wouldn't run – and Yani had stated his intentions very clearly. If the bookshops didn't run, he would continue his journey across the country except now he would focus on the city centres. The potential for chaos was unimaginable.

It was around this time that I took up my old profession. I hadn't worked as a bookseller since 1997, which was when I had known Yani. 'Known' may be overstating our acquain-tance – which was just that. Yani was a figure I was familiar with mainly from the small staffroom in the newer part of the shop. I remember he brought his lunch in Tupperware – baked beans, baked potatoes, occasional stews which he would heat up in the polythene-scented microwave oven that we all shared. He would sit, with his steaming lunchbox bal-anced on the edge of the small table in the middle of the room, reading a folded copy of the *Bookseller* or perhaps one of the Sunday review sections – often, depressingly, on the Tuesday or Wednesday after its publication. Something about this irritated me. Yani had no great love for his job, or certainly had never declared any, and thus I assumed this behaviour was an affectation, with something inauthentic and obedient about it, as if he were cowed by the nearby presence of managers and assistant managers, or maybe even the spectre of Head Office which leered down from the noticeboard in the form of photocopied announcements and directives. To me all these were joke figures. My presence in the shop was purely temporary – I was an artist, a painter, on my way to warmer climes – and I paid no more attention to those authorities than a sixth former about to leave school does to his teachers. But Yani was not me. This was his job. There was no grand plan it was supporting. This was his life.

Those days were many – those shared lunchtimes alone in the cramped, malodorous staffroom. Did Yani know that I thought myself better than him? I suspected that he might. I would smile tightly at him on occasions. And there came a time when he tried to talk to me. He began a conversation about the situation in the stockroom. The two unpackers who worked there were disgruntled and mutinous – engaged in a dispute over their conditions and perceived lack of support. Cases of books were piling up high, and new stock was not making it out on to the shop floor. Yani tried to make a joke – to begin some banter. I felt something curl up inside, repelled at his attempt at familiarity. I smiled and looked down at my food. He continued: 'Not going to have any books to sell – at this rate.'

I nodded at him.

'Eh, Ian? They'll have to do something about it then. They'll be in real trouble.'

'They will, Yani.' I looked down at my copy of *The Face*, turning the page, and shifting slightly towards the wall and away from him.

He muttered something into his Tupperware, mixing the chopped-up sausages into the beans. As a result of my rebuttal he was trying to make it seem like he had always intended the conversation to be with no one but himself. I felt no need to disabuse him of this apprehension.

There were other times when I could have spoken to him, engaged with him, shared a simple conversation – but I chose not to. We often went for a drink after work at the Lamb and Flag, particularly on Friday and Saturday nights. The atmosphere could be fun – quite raucous. Much mocking of management – who would be in attendance too and would happily absorb what came their way. Some intrigue and gossip – a staff comprised of mainly young, mainly single, or at least unmarried, people were inevitably going to couple quite liberally. I enjoyed – at least most of the time – being part of this fray. I had more than one assignation myself with a member of staff and it relieved the ennui that could attend the job. It was one of these nights that I saw Yani, off to one side, alone at a table. Maybe not courageous enough to fully join the party himself, but sitting close enough to indicate that he had some association with this crowd. I knew it would have taken Yani considerable effort just to attend that night, to make it into this company. It was far from his natural territory. He attempted a smile, raised his glass at me. Was he offering to buy me a drink? I turned away, engaging even deeper in the conversation I was having. After that night I don't recall seeing Yani in the pub again.

Sometimes, I have to admit, I found myself wondering about Yani's life beyond work. I knew he lived somewhere in south London – in one of those areas where you had to catch two buses just to get to a mainline station, which would still only get you into Waterloo. I assumed he had no romantic connections. I wasn't aware of any hobbies. Once I'd left the shop I never thought about him again. The shock of recognition, when I saw his face on *News at Ten*, accounted for this being the only moment that I can ever remember thinking my waking life must in fact have been a dream.

I took up my old job because of the money. With the new rates I could earn in three months what I was making in a year. There would be no impact on my creativity. I was only selling my time. The advantage of bookselling – at least formerly – was that it was a stressless occupation. One picked it up in the morning upon passing through the shop doors and left it there in the evening on the way out. The only discomforts came from the inevitable boredoms that could sometimes occur and the more menial aspects – unpacking, fetching and carrying. Now, with this new salary, the freedom it bought was a wonder. There was, of course, a new stress. Yani's method of management was revealed to be predicated on surprise. Though the bookshops had essentially become churches – divorced from all commercial obligations – it was clear that Yani wanted them run better than they had ever been before. Certainly to go in a branch of Waterstone's was to encounter a state of perfection. Yani's regime of unexpected visits maintained this order. If he found anything out of place, or anything that displeased him, the individual who was perceived as being responsible died. Not in agony as his civilian victims had – a bookseller for over twenty years Yani obviously felt some comradeship with his staff – but instantaneously and with devastating suddenness. I would not be speaking the truth if I said that this matter was of no concern to me. However, sales of my paintings had diminished to a slow dribble that would not sustain my living costs. I had a young wife to support – and the idea of a job that would generously cover all expenses and leave me time and energy enough to create freely was too tempting to turn away from. Rachel agreed, and because she knew me to be quite meticulous by nature she thought the risk of provoking Yani's displeasure was minimal. After I'd been working there for two months we came up with a plan. It was amazing how quickly one was able to push knowledge of

Yani's merciless regime away from one's daily consciousness. If Rachel started working there too, within a year we could have saved enough for us both to live on for another three, or maybe even four. It would give me time to put together a new collection of work, work that I really wanted to do. I was sure that if I followed this course, the work would be strong and more appealing to a buyer than the stuff that was coming out of the more fearful, desperate place I had been creating from in recent years.

I was not, at that point, afraid of what Yani might do to me and Rachel. The rate of deaths had dropped in recent years. And the sense of camaraderie and mutual respect between staff was in vivid contrast to the casual griping and dissatisfaction that I remembered from my previous engagement.

Rachel was younger than me, wiser than me. In many ways she had saved me. Saved me from myself. A life of casual and imprudent relationships with women – begun without thought or reflection – with sex as the trigger. That was how I had characterised them to myself in the past but it was worse than that. I had equated sex and sexual conquest with achievement. That was what guided me, an attempt to prove something presumably to the rest of the world – maybe to show I was something better than the likes of Yani. Yes, Rachel was attractive, beautiful even. But something in her shone and that pulled me towards her even more than her physicality. She changed my work too – it became sunnier, clearer, more generous. It was only recently that this had begun to change back, which may explain why I was no longer prospering. The darkness, the rejection of others, the desire to withdraw. This was a gravity in me that I found impossible to resist.

Rachel and I had been to lunch. Our branch was in a large new shopping centre on the edge of York. We'd been there for about seven months. We both loved the city – vibrant now, with a vital culture, but with deep roots that were visible everywhere you walked. I even secretly liked the Stonebrick

Centre, the out of town shopping arcade where we worked. We ambled back happily – not yet late – but with only four or five minutes of our lunch hour left. When we entered the shop it was as quiet as an examination room. I realised straight away of course that Yani was there. Within seconds of knowing this I caught a flash of his bright floral-patterned shirt among the silent shelves. In that instant I was shocked but also excited and terrified. My first thoughts were of my section. Naturally enough I was in charge of the art books – this included architecture, cinema and music. Was everything shelved? Was everything unpacked? Was everything priced? Only when these questions had been answered did I think about Rachel.

'Is your section tidy?'

'Yes,' she said. I listened for fear in her voice, but heard only a steady calmness. The answer is what I would have expected. She was even more meticulous than me – which was one of the reasons I never worried about her fate here. 'We're not late,' she said, risking a quick glance at her watch. It was true – we still had two minutes before we were due back on the shop floor. I guessed that she was worrying about me. 'Come on.' She touched my forearm and led me in the direction of the staffroom, which was close to the rear entrance of the shop that we had just come in through.

Aware of my racing heart I punched the entry code into the secure latch and pulled the door open. I threw my coat off and on to the nearest available peg. Rachel hung hers up with quiet grace. We headed back out to the shop floor being conscious to not walk too close together. There was nothing forbidden about relations between staff but it was not acceptable for there to be any affection discernible to the book-buying public. I could see Dave Brimley, the assistant manager, standing at the centre till. He was tidying the pens at the side of the monitor screens. His hands were visibly shaking. I willed him to stay calm. Rachel was already at the gardening section. Her first bookcase contained gardening reference books. They abutted the end of my film directors' biographies. Orson Welles stared from a face-out display.

We had drilled for this day. You were supposed to engage yourself in some meaningful yet neutral activity while awaiting Yani's appraisal. There was a small skip over by the dumb-waiter that happened to be in the corner of my section. It was a means of getting the books up and down to the unpacking room. I walked over to it with the idea that I could begin distributing its contents in a natural and reasonable manner. I could hear the mutter of low conversation. Here, rounding the corner from mind body spirit, was Edwina – the manager – and Yani himself. She glanced in my direction then looked away. The pair paused before a set-up of display bins. I saw Rachel, opposite me, reorganising titles on a shelf – moving the taller books to one end. I looked over to the next section – sport – and saw Andrew Wiltshire, the young buyer who was also a semi-professional tennis player, standing stiffly by his football section like a soldier in a sentry box. I risked a flick of the eyes in Yani's direction. He was a huge figure – at least double the size of the one I remembered. His bright shirt hung round his belly like curtaining. He had crossed the line of normal human proportions into something verging on the freakish. His bearded face was not dissimilar, however. I wondered if he would remember me, and the thought was accompanied by a sort of pride – pride at the fact that I had known Yani when he was just a man.

Rachel was still organising her shelves, intently focused on the activity she had set herself. If we both just kept our attention on whatever our legitimate tasks were Yani would be gone, the moment would pass, and our positions would be secure. He would not visit again for some considerable time and by then we would be retired, away in South America or New Zealand, living on our savings, establishing our renaissance exactly as we had planned it. I looked up again. Yani had finished his low conversation with Edwina. He turned sharply and began walking towards us. Edwina turned too, following. Yani's eyes were fixed either on me or on the books directly behind me. I felt the adrenaline rising and burning. I wanted to please him, in that moment. I wanted Yani to know I was good. He was still looking. There was nothing on his face to indicate whether he remembered me, whether the fact that we had known each other even flickered on his consciousness. Without slowing, he turned to Edwina and began talking again, his voice quiet, the words inaudible. He was different in almost every way from the Yani of memory. This Yani had authority, purpose. Perhaps the one thing that remained, that was discernible, was a thread of that commitment to his task – the one I had labelled as being ersatz. It did not seem so now. As they approached, Yani swerved sharply to the right. He paused before Rachel, who turned to face him. She lowered her head respectfully, then raised it again slowly. Yani glanced back at me, giving me the most cursory look, then back to Rachel. Without pausing in his speech he raised his hand and crooked his finger. An assistant ran forward – a teenage boy who had been walking behind him – and placed a small white towel on Rachel's shoulder. Yani crooked his finger again and without any intervening event my wife collapsed to the floor, clutching her stomach, yelling in abrupt pain.

I heard myself scream before I knew I had done so. The moment froze. Rachel rolling on the floor – Yani's pitiless bulk above her, the teenage boy hovering, Edwina whitefaced. Yani shrugged his shoulders.

'Please,' I said. He looked at me. I looked into his heavily-lidded eyes, searched in that moment for something I could connect with, a thread of shared humanity. 'Please,' I said again – shouting this time. I found I was kneeling before Yani in the middle of the shop floor. Gladly kneeling. I shuffled – like a child, like a toddler, the tears already at my eyes. 'Please.' Yani turned slightly, didn't really look at me, turned back. 'Please,' I said once more, feeling myself emptying into the word. Yani raised his hand casually. Crooked his finger again. Rachel opened her mouth, sucked in a great gulp of air, let out a cry. She had wet herself, I noticed. She sat up. Her breathing was fast. She took me in, on the floor, on my knees. Slowly she stood up. Yani sniffed, placed the heel of his thumb against his forehead for a moment. And then he walked off, without looking at me again, his shirt swinging around his enormous bulk. Other members of staff were trying not to react, but I saw them looking excitedly and nervously in our direction.

Yani left our branch without taking any life. Perhaps he enjoyed making the occasional act of clemency. No one had ever spoken of such a thing before.

To ask for mercy and receive it. The experience was new to me. It haunts me still. To be in such debt. Rachel will not, will never speak of it. Even now, she is silent much of the time, her sun permanently clouded.

And Yani walks on.

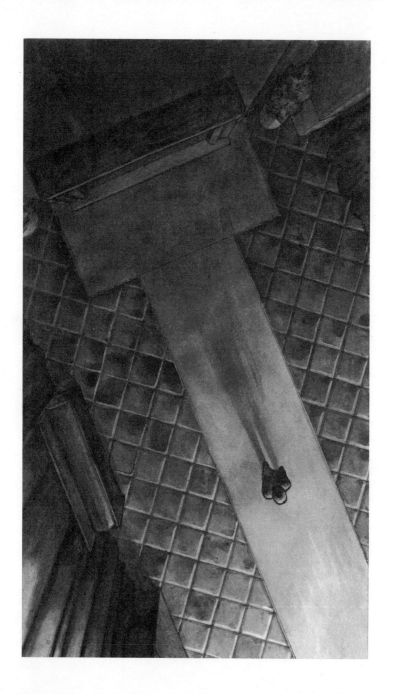

The Challenge Club

Of course Crabbe had heard of the Challenge Club – but he had never expected anyone to invite him to attend.

'Do you want to meet me at the Challenge, about eight,' Tommy Redknapp had said as lightly as if he were arranging an assignation at Starbucks.

'You mean, you can just walk in?' The lack of knowledge about the club's etiquette was a confession that in some circles might be considered unacceptably gauche. Crabbe, however, thought of Tommy as a friend.

'You're my guest. I will sign you in,' said Tommy, as if this were the most obvious thing in the world.

'But the dinner jacket? The dicky bow?' Crabbe did a little cuckoo whistle and waggled his fingers over his breastbone.

Tommy shook his head. 'You're not a member. Don't need to worry about that. Smart, though, if you can. You'll feel better with a tie on.'

Crabbe walked along the Soho streets in the general direction of Jekyll Court, where he knew the Challenge Club to be located, though he had never been there before, never even dared to walk past. It was cold for April and his breath clouded pleasingly in front of him as he strode along. He had to admit to a certain excitement. There was a dim sense that he was being admitted to a world he had no right even to visit. Somewhere inside – if he probed deep enough – was a feeling that he would never be worthy of membership of such an institution. But to be allowed a look even. A glimpse within. For a brief moment he rose higher in his own estimation. Of course no one would mistake him for a member. But they might see him as someone who was fit to associate with others who were.

He'd rung his wife about it as soon as he could.

'You're not going, are you?'

'Why not?'

Siobhan's laugh rattled in his ear. 'Come on! All that dressing up.'

'I only have to put a tie on.'

'And the small matter of it being men only. In this day and age.'

'Women can go too.'

'But they can't join, can they, Justin. They can't be members.'

'I'm only meeting Tommy.'

'You could meet him anywhere.'

'I want to see what it's like inside. Don't you?'

'Not really.'

A pause. Crabbe inserted his finger into the coiled cable that dangled from the phone's receiver. He wiggled it around idly animating the plastic spiral.

'Well, go then,' she said after a moment of silence in which Crabbe had wanted her to be more excited. She must have sensed his disappointment for when she spoke again her words were lighter, her customary giggle more discernible. 'Enjoy it if you must. But it's silly. You know that, don't you.'

'Silly things can be fun,' he said.

The Challenge Club had not been open six months. The whole venture was driven by the actor Henry Boardman. He wanted to create a haven for creative people in the heart of Soho that would show up all previous attempts to do so for the counterfeit enterprises he considered them to be. Boardman had a vision – inspired, so he said, by a dream. A place of enchantment, of theatre, that would fuel the imagination of everyone who stepped inside it. Yes, the Challenge paid homage to the great Victorian clubs on which much of London life was founded (hence the bizarre and retrogressive membership rules), but it was also forward-looking, building something new and intoxicating behind the Georgian brick façades, between the crowding edit suites, sound facilities and production companies. Boardman's project was financed by a mysterious Russian – an oligarch called Yevgeny Grigorovich who Boardman had met on the set of an adaptation of Dostoevsky's novella *The Double* which the Russian was producing. And the day work began on the club, Boardman, who was a notable talent, particularly on the London stage, abandoned his acting career and devoted himself completely to his dream. The rumours began circulating through Soho months before the Challenge Club opened its doors: that membership would be by invitation only; that annual fees would be in excess of three hundred thousand pounds; that all the serving staff would be eunuchs. Every one of these was of course pure nonsense, but the club did have exclusive criteria in place, and Boardman personally approved – or declined – every single member.

There were journalists with fingers poised over laptop keyboards ready to destroy the club's reputation from its opening night onwards but as yet no one had been able to land a truly devastating blow. Disconcertingly – as far as the newspapers and magazines were concerned – the wit and charm and chutzpah of the place seemed to win over even the most cynical columnist. Additionally, all of the capital's editors – both red-top and broadsheet – were members, which may have inhibited the running of any really derogatory story.

For Crabbe all this was of secondary interest. The thing that engaged him most about the Challenge Club was the glamour, the excitement, the magic. From being a child – sitting on his Grandma Russell's knee watching the Royal

Variety show, staying up late for *Parkinson* on Saturdays, or school trips to London hoping to catch a glimpse of a famous person – the notion of celebrity and its attendant romance had enchanted him, dazzled him. The sense that these people were special, people you wanted to know, people you wished knew you. Clever, witty, delightful people, with something elevated about them, something that differentiated them from the more mundane individuals who surrounded Crabbe and his family. It was as if they courted their own spotlight wherever they went and if you stood near them a bit of that light might catch you, lifting you on to another plane that was about something more than buses and Morrisons and boring Sunday afternoons.

Given that this glitter flowed freely in Crabbe's veins it might have indicated a career path that would take him somewhere near stage or cameras. However, Crabbe's father – a professional man from a line of professional men – insisted that Crabbe subscribe to a profession himself. And since Crabbe had never been able to identify any ability that would qualify him for a performance-related career (or perhaps had never been encouraged to), it is no surprise that he ended up in that most maligned of all the professions: accountancy.

The joke about accountancy was that it was boring, but Crabbe did not find it so. A well-balanced spreadsheet, a clever solution to a tax problem, the steady liturgy of quarterly VAT and twelve-monthly income tax returns, all these things gave him a solid and sustaining pleasure. And strangely, through no conscious effort on his part, Crabbe found that he began to acquire a number of clients with some connection to showbusiness, and then, through these, a number who were what one might actually call famous – among them the comedian and panel show regular Tommy Redknapp. He was a naturally funny, lively and gregarious individual who had welcomed Crabbe into his Dartmouth Park home as a friend as well as an accountant. They had even been out together to the theatre, mutually drawn by a love of old variety and music hall acts. True, Tommy usually wanted to talk business in some way, but it was always in a friendly manner, and he had a way of sparking things up so his questions about cash-flow and tax planning sounded like games, opportunities to spar, to make jokes, to crack the air with wit. Crabbe was aware of a strategic element to this on Tommy's part – Redknapp got more advice for free than perhaps, as a professional man, Crabbe should allow. But he knew he was getting something in return and it felt enough like friendship to counter any doubts Crabbe had that his goodwill was being exploited.

Arriving at the turning into Jekyll Court – a tiny alleyway hidden away at the end of Richmond Mews – Crabbe felt his heart quicken. His stomach gave a little lurch. He felt like he was about to walk on stage. Suddenly he wanted to turn around, flee the way he had come. What was he frightened of? Not being good enough? Being revealed to be less than others? But this was ridiculous. He was going to see Tommy, to sit with a friend, sip a glass of red wine. Nothing more would be demanded of him. It was a professional assignation. Think of it like that. A business meeting. He was an adult, accomplished in his sphere. It was all he had to remember.

And here was the door – anonymous, heavy, with two black lacquered panels – interlocking 'C's carved into their centres. Standing before it Crabbe had a vision of himself as C-3PO cowering outside Jabba the Hutt's palace in *Return of the Jedi*. He shook his head to dispel the ridiculous image. He was not even a fan of the film. He searched the doorpost to his left and found the little metal box – a tiny camera embedded at its top. He pushed the buzzer. It made no sound. Maybe it wasn't working. He peered into the lens, as if he might see something through it. Nothing. Reluctantly he pushed the buzzer again. A sudden burst of tinny static brought the inscrutable speaker-box to life.

'Challenge,' it said. Crabbe couldn't tell if the owner of the voice was male or female.

'Yes. Hello . . .' Crabbe halted, stuttering, as if he were a time-traveller from the eighteenth century, unfamiliar with the accursed black magic of entryphones. He struggled to control his voice, took a deep breath and began again. 'I'm here to see Tommy Redknapp.' An absurd pause, loaded with imagined menace, in which Crabbe felt himself being scrutinised by the implacable eye of the security camera. Another pop of white noise, followed by an elongated buzz. Then the click of a remotely operated latch. Ignoring the fluttering hollowness in his stomach, Crabbe pushed at the lacquered wood. He panicked that the brief sliver of time which the buzz afforded him would end before he had a chance to get the ludicrously heavy door open. He did, however, manage it and made his way within.

The first thing he was aware of was the smell. New carpets, wax polish, pine needles, wood smoke. The vestibule beyond the entrance was dark, like chocolate of the finest quality. Inlaid into the red majolica-tiled floor, a line of rush matting. Heavy velvet curtains hung on either side. Round a corner, curved an enormous returning staircase. In the centre of the square hallway, rising all the way to the ceiling several storeys above, stood a towering spruce tree. There was no indication as to how it had got there. It was not potted. Rather it seemed to be growing through an exposed panel of earth, straight from the ground. Given the month it was safe to say this arboreal feature had nothing to do with Christmas. It must have been a permanent fixture. As Crabbe mounted the polished wooden stairs he breathed in and savoured the heavy scent of the tree's branches. The expansive walls – which one might have expected to see hung with paintings or framed posters – were completely unadorned, a simple scrubbed hardwood. A low purr of conversation came from somewhere above, the volume rising as Crabbe climbed. Arriving on the first landing he was faced with a large kneehole desk in the French style, placed, somewhat unusually, in the centre of the floor. Behind it sat a busy-looking young woman with an immaculately cut bobbed hairdo. She looked up and smiled disarmingly.

'I'm here to meet someone,' said Crabbe, though it was more of a throaty whisper than actual speech.

'Of course, sir. Who are you meeting?' said the girl, her voice rising interrogatively. Crabbe's hand rose to his collar to check his tie. For a chill moment he thought he might have forgotten to put it on.

'Er . . . Tommy Redknapp. Mr Redknapp.' She looked down at her appointment book, running an elegantly manicured finger down the page. Crabbe noted the delicacy of the handwriting therein – a slanting antique script that would not have looked out of place in an eighteenth-century diary.

'Mr Crabbe, is it?'

'Yes,' he said eagerly.

'If you could go up to Max Miller. Mr Redknapp is waiting for you there.'

'Fine, thank you,' said Crabbe, relieved not to have been rejected. It was only as he turned and glanced at the various doorways and the enormous stairway which climbed for at least another two floors that he realised his destination was not obvious. There was a brief internal debate about whether it would be OK to turn around and ask for clarification. Stop being such a child, he told himself firmly.

'Excuse me,' he said, turning round as confidently as he could. The young woman was already looking down again, writing handsome calligraphy in her notebook. She looked up. She was impossibly beautiful. 'I . . . I haven't, er, been, um . . . Where is the . . .?'

'Max Miller?'

'Yes.'

'Up the stairs, through the curtain, then up the narrow staircase, at the top on your left.'

'Thank you. Thank you.'

The girl smiled briefly.

And so up another flight, round a landing – glimpses into fire-lit rooms, leather sofas, arms dangling loosely over their sides. Laughter and conversation. A man in full evening dress descending the stairs ahead of him. 'Don't cross on the stairs,' Crabbe's mother always used to warn him. These were so wide there was probably a special dispensation that neutralised any such superstition. At the top on the landing was a row of display cabinets. It was hard to judge from this distance exactly what they contained. As Crabbe approached the disparate items began to resolve themselves. A grand-looking felt hat. A futuristic gun. A sheet of glass with what looked like a photograph of a black, gothic-looking castle mounted upon it. Crabbe paused in front of the display. Close up he could see stitching on the hat where it had been unevenly repaired; the gun, which had appeared to be metal from a distance, revealed itself to be made of wood and flaking paint; and the clearly delineated photograph of the castle turned out in fact to be a blurry and impressionistic painting. Crabbe peered at this, trying to make retrospective sense of the illusion.

'Dracula's castle.'

Crabbe whirled around. Behind him stood a tall man whom he vaguely recognised. He too was in full evening dress, though a shiny, mother of pearl-coloured waistcoat peeked out playfully from under his jacket.

'Dracula's castle,' the man said again. He was in his early forties, with closely cropped grey hair. He had a bright and alive face, glowing with vigour and purpose. 'Painted by Les Bowie in 1963. It's a matte painting.'

'Matte painting,' said Crabbe, curious. He'd heard the term but couldn't remember what it referred to.

'You know. From old movies.' The man clapped a hand on Crabbe's shoulder. He wore two signet rings, one of bright gold and one of platinum. 'They'd build a little bit of set and paint the rest. Line up the camera. Put that glass in front of it and wham – Dracula's castle sitting on a hill. Bloody marvellous.

Don't you think? All computers these days of course. Not the same thing at all. What you going to put on display now? A CD-ROM?' He smiled sadly, patted Crabbe's shoulder and walked off, calling back as he departed, 'You haven't got a drink. Get yourself a drink, man.' Crabbe watched him go. He looked at his watch, and realised he was now nearly five minutes late. A little flash of panic at the thought that Tommy might be displeased, impatiently waiting for him, made Crabbe turn away from the display and walk speedily towards the curtain, which hung below a picture of Max Miller. As he got closer he could see that this picture, though it looked like a silkscreened Warhol-style print, was in fact made up of marquetry inlaid into the wood panelling.

Music was audible now, an arrangement of Dave Brubeck's 'Blue Rondo à la Turk'. Crabbe was surprised to see as he entered the room, not only that the music was being played live, but that the small band, sitting on a raised dais at the side of the room in front of him, was made up of boys in their early teens. They played immaculately. Visible over their shoulders, perched on a bar stool, tapping out the six-eight tempo with the edge of a champagne glass, was Tommy Redknapp, smiling gently, his bright-blue eyes idly sweeping the room. He picked up Crabbe's presence. His smile broadened. He waved his glass in the air. Crabbe crossed a modest elevated dance-floor in order to reach the bar where Tommy sat. He felt exposed as he did so, as if everyone would be scrutinising him. In fact no one in the lightly populated room responded in any perceptible way.

'Crabcake, how hell you?' Tommy held out his hand in a relaxed manner. Crabbe shook it warmly.

'Nice place.'

'Damn sight nicer than the other places, that's for sure. Drink?'

'Just a mineral water.'

Tommy looked at him sceptically.

'A Bloody Mary, then.'

'Good man. Good man. Olives? Bombay mix? Wotsits?'

'Wotsits?'

'Wotsits. Quavers. Frazzles. You can get anything at the Challenge.'

Crabbe thought for a moment. 'Just some olives.' Tommy gave him another sceptical look. 'Frazzles, then, please.'

'Bloody Mary, another champagne, and a bowl of Frazzles, please,' Tommy said to the bar-girl.

'And this is Vitro.'

'Vitro?'

'It's the theatre.'

'There's a theatre?'

'It's only small.'

'They don't put on shows?'

'Sometimes. Mainly it's smaller scale things. Rehearsed readings. Good place for assorted members to try their stuff out. Screen too. Up there. Comes down. They have film shows. All sorts of things.'

They pushed through a pair of plush-covered double doors into a modestly sized but beautifully detailed auditorium. Crabbe remembered being nine years old. Saturday mornings. There'd been a movie club at the ABC where they showed Children's Film Foundation films and old cartoons. He'd begged to be allowed to go. His mother hadn't wanted him to. She never said why but he assumed that she thought it was common, like all the other fun things that were forbidden. And then one week on a Thursday shopping trip there'd been an advert for a double bill: '*A Hitch in Time* and *Mr Horatio Knibbles*'. Something about the combination of a giant rabbit and a man who used to be Doctor Who together on a poster was utterly irresistible. And so, uncharacteristically, Crabbe had wheedled and whined and schmoozed until he got what he wanted and permission was given.

His father had dropped him outside the ABC on Foregate Street and he went in, clutching a five-pound note, feeling impossibly old and suddenly apprehensive at what lay beyond the mustard-yellow, portholed doors at the far end of the foyer.

Ticket in hand he'd dared to purchase a box of sweets – Paynes Poppets. At first it was going to be Fruit Gums. The boxed ones were shaped like segments of the fruit they took their flavour from, but then Crabbe had decided that they were too similar to those he would have been allowed normally – at least on special occasions. He wanted to enjoy something completely novel. He'd never seen Paynes Poppets anywhere outside a cinema. And had he been with either of his parents it was a pleasure that would have been denied him. The chocolate would have been deemed cheap or unpleasant or unhealthy or unsuitable and thus not worthy of the fifty pence which – as a coda – would have been declared absurdly exorbitant.

Holding the box tightly – an unknown pleasure that might be snatched from him at any moment – Crabbe had pushed through the double doors and gone inside.

The auditorium roared with the sound of unrestrained joy. Boys rocketed around the perimeters of the raked seating, girls shrieked from the balcony above. Plastic cartons of Kia-Ora and balled-up sweet papers flew repeatedly in the air, bursting into light in the projector's beam – the massive ghosts of their disrupting shadows on the screen provoking momentary howls of delight as they rose and fell.

Quietly, not wanting to draw attention to himself, Crabbe had found a seat, close to one of the centre aisles, towards the rear. He could smell cigarette smoke and thought at first there must be an adult there. Maybe that was what had drawn him in that direction. He risked a glance behind. Three boys were huddled, two rows back, lit by the fluctuating glow of a fag. One of them snarled at Crabbe, like a provoked dog. Immediately he flicked his head forward to the screen. It was a scene with a policeman, questioning some children. A percussive round of stamping began, originating in the circle balcony above and ricocheting around until the entire audience was joining in. Aware of his aloneness, sensing in his gut the fraudulence of the act, Crabbe nevertheless tried stamping himself. He thought it might unleash something, some pleasure that would connect him with the happy, living, raucousness around him. He just felt uncomfortable and stopped. Something stung him in the back of the neck. He didn't turn round to find its source.

He sat there rigidly for the next ten minutes of *Mr Horatio Knibbles* and then surprising himself he strode out of the cinema, still clutching his Poppets. The rest of the morning was spent in the adjacent Wimpy Bar nursing a Horlicks and joylessly reading and rereading a *TV Comic* bought from the newsagents next door until the time came for his pre-arranged pick up. Then he stood dishonestly outside the ABC, waiting for the green Fiat to roll around the corner and collect him. He never went to the Saturday Morning Minors again.

They were sitting in an upstairs dining area of the Challenge Club – modelled on a Golden Egg café from the 1960s. All gaudy moulded fibreglass and bright abstract prints. The intensity of the colour scheme was intimidating, but invigorating too. Opposite Crabbe, two tables away, sat an actress Crabbe recognised from the television show *Casualty*. She was very pretty – a kind of prettiness he was not used to seeing in real life. There was something magnetic about it. One had to look.

'What you staring at?' said Tommy Redknapp, his open mouth revealing a mess of half-chewed sausage and egg.

'Nothing,' said Crabbe, suddenly slightly ashamed.

Grinning, Redknapp turned round, turning back immediately.

'Yeah. Isn't she.' Another forkful loaded with three fat chips, piled on top of the as yet unswallowed sausage and egg. 'You should have been here for her life-drawing session.'

'What?' said Crabbe, wondering if he'd heard right.

'They run these life-drawing classes. You don't need to be any good at it. Just another of their schemes to unleash your innate creativity.' Redknapp drew inverted commas in the air around the last two words. 'A perk of membership.' He picked up a chip and dipped it in the little tub of mayonnaise in front of him. 'Anyway members are encouraged to model.' Redknapp paused slightly for effect before raising his eyebrows up and down suggestively. 'Trouble is, you don't know who's going to be modelling before you go. You could be sat in front of some great fat arse for two hours. Bad form to get up and go if you don't fancy the goods on offer.' Crabbe tried to swallow. His mouth had gone dry and he was aware of a slight tremble in his hands. He kept them firmly on his lap. 'It's a numbers game. Go enough and you're bound to see something interesting. You might even get good at drawing.'

'Have you . . . ?' said Crabbe, attempting a casual interest.

'Oh yes,' was all Redknapp said, smiling enigmatically.

They were walking along the side of a subterranean pool area called the Canal when Redknapp asked Crabbe if he would like to join. The redbrick walls and ceiling were dappled with smoothly shifting patches, the reflections of pinprick lights inlaid into the tiles beneath the water. A verge of what appeared to be real grass lined the opposite side of the room. A few people were sitting there, spread out reading books and papers. They didn't react in any way as Crabbe and Redknapp walked by, taking their places on the underground lawn.

'They're having a numbers drive. Like a rights issue. I guess they're short of funds. Anyway – existing members have all been asked to pitch in. If they know anybody.'

'They wouldn't want me,' said Crabbe. It was a thought released and the minute that he heard it echoing off the brick walls around and above him he felt uncomfortable that it had been verbalised.

'Mate,' said Redknapp, looking at him with furrowed brow. 'What are you talking about?'

Crabbe tried to laugh, as if the statement had in some way been a joke. He wished he hadn't said it. Redknapp studied him for a minute.

'Because you think you're a muggle?' Redknapp shook his head. 'You're not a muggle.' He pulled at a tuft of grass in front of him. It came up, a tiny root system visible in the knot of earth at its base. 'You're one of us. In the game.' The comedian rolled the bit of vegetation idly between his fingers and flicked it towards the canal. 'Come on in. The water's lovely.' Crabbe leaned back, looked up at the ceiling. Three huge UV bulbs beat down their light at him.

As he walked towards his home on Gillespie Road, Crabbe found he was still digesting Tommy Redknapp's offer. Part of him was excited – more than excited, delighted – to be considered worthy of membership. Once a Scottish client had insisted on paying for Crabbe's visits to Falkirk and made sure all the tickets were first class. The sense of pride mingled with specialness that Crabbe had experienced as he stretched out his feet and sipped at the complimentary coffee was akin to what he was feeling now. But something else accompanied it, a tarnish to the chrome, and it was something like a burden, a subtle weight. As he reached the front gate of number thirty-two, the neat little garden in the yard, the scratched but polished knocker resting on the front door, the simple pleasure they gave him seemed in direct contrast to the opulence he had just spent the evening experiencing.

'You don't really want to join though. Do you?' Siobhan was in bed, looking up at him.

'No, not really.' Was that the truth? He slid in next to her, caught the smell of her hair and clean white T-shirt. 'It was all a little over the top.'

She put down her book. 'Still, nice of him to ask you, I suppose. He certainly didn't have to.' For a moment Crabbe found himself thinking of the actress in the café bar – unclothed on satin cushions. 'How much?' said Siobhan.

'Hmm?'

'How much does it cost? To join?'

'Five hundred or something,' he said. It was in fact twelve hundred.

'Well, that settles it, I should think. Be better off with a couple of nights in a nice hotel.'

Crabbe nodded, though he didn't know if Siobhan saw in the semi-dark of the room.

As he sat before the easel with a pencil he tried to remember the last time he had done so. Fourteen years old? Fifteen? It must have been art O Level. The practical exam. An upright floor polisher – its flex wrapped chaotically around its battered metal body. He hadn't thought he'd been any good. As the exam finished he'd wondered if he'd glimpsed something interesting in the imperfections of his lines – the way a particular bend or kink had been exaggerated by how he'd seen it. For a moment he almost thought the drawing was good. He shook his head and the hum of disappointment had resumed. It had been confirmed by the C grade he had received.

And now here he was, twenty-five years later, with a 3B in one hand and a Staedtler rubber in the other, waiting for a life model to enter. Tommy Redknapp nudged him. There was a movement by the door. Part of the attraction, that surely accounted for the popularity of the class, was the weekly surprise of who would be posing. Crabbe risked a glance around the room, though not at his classmates – he still felt too self-conscious and uncertain to dare eye-contact. Rather he was taking in the drawings mounted on the walls. This too reminded him of school, as a number of them – the best of them – were neatly framed. Others were just tacked up with pins. Occasionally one could recognise a face – a member of the cast of *EastEnders*, a producer or writer of some renown – but mostly they were of portions of limbs, of flesh, buttocks, breasts.

'Here we go,' said Tommy. 'Eyes down for a full house.' Crabbe stifled a nervous laugh. He was grateful for Tommy at his side, the legitimacy this loaned him.

A flash of kimono at the door. Crabbe looked down. His hand was trembling. He pressed the point of the pencil into his leg until it hurt. He wasn't going to look up until the figure was in place, whoever they may be. The bright colour of the silk in his peripheral vision. A rustle of fabric falling. The figure was close to him. He could feel heat.

The first impression was of hair. Not head hair. Body hair, an abundance of it. And bulk. It was like an animal in a farmyard. Weight, bulk, hair, heat. There were breasts but they belonged to a man. Loose, fleshy, nothing globular, just weight and sag. The face was bearded, older. A distinguished and familiar character actor. Because of how he had arranged himself he was directly facing Crabbe. The actor shifted slightly on his cushions. He opened his legs, thighs massive like hirsute Christmas hams. He shuffled his hips forward angling purposefully at Crabbe the black nest of his pubic hair– three pink eggs just visible within. Crabbe looked nervously to his left. Next to him, on the other side of Tommy, was a serious-looking man in his early thirties. He had a small red plastic toolbox on the seat next to him. It was full of pencils, rubbers, cloths, pens, coloured inks and brushes. The man pushed his small, rectangular glasses up his nose and removed a stick of charcoal from the box. Next to him was a woman – elfin but curvy, perhaps in her early thirties. She was looking at Crabbe. He must have appeared comically frightened or nervous because she was on the edge of laughter. She saw he was looking at her, saw his discomfort. Her expression warmed. Crabbe turned back to the blank sheet of A2 sugar paper in front of him.

'Fuck me,' said Tommy, barely audibly. 'This is a three-pencil job.'

Crabbe reached out with his right hand and began to draw.

*

Afterwards a number of the art club attendees had arranged to meet in the dining area for a drink or a milkshake – or a combination of the two: Noggin the Nog was a powerful concoction somewhere between advocaat, Baileys and a Frappuccino. Crabbe had no intention of sampling one but then Tommy brought him one anyway. He sipped at it suspiciously. The word that came into his head as the cold, milky liquid ran on to his tongue was 'divine'.

'I think that was the funniest thing I've ever seen.' Standing next to Crabbe, with a glass of iced tea in her slender hand, was the elfin-looking woman from the studio. Crabbe felt himself blushing.

'I'm sorry.' The music wasn't loud in the dining area, but he felt himself shouting. He worried about his breath, whether it might smell, and he took another gulp of Noggin trying to swill it a little as he swallowed.

'Your face – when old George Dunning opened his legs.' She was cheeky, impish, grinning up at him. He was nearly a foot taller than her.

'I . . . I . . .' Crabbe didn't know what to say.

'I'm teasing. I'm sorry.' She looked contrite. 'I'm Davina. Carol Skinner's wife.' For a moment the feminine name confused Crabbe. Then he remembered that Skinner was a television presenter – a male television presenter currently enjoying some success in America with his scabrous chat show. Crabbe looked around the room. 'He's not here,' she said, seeing this. 'He's in New York. I'm Russell Hird's guest.' She nodded to a man by the bar holding an old-fashioned pint glass laughing with two other men. Clearly one of them had just told a dirty joke. She turned back to face Crabbe. 'Forgive me for saying, but you don't look like the others.' Crabbe felt himself blush again. 'I'm sorry,' said Davina again, obviously registering his discomfort. 'What I meant to say is I thought you were the teacher – at first. The last time I went to one of these things there was a teacher. And you didn't seem like one of those other arses who's clearly just come to gawp. Like Tommy Redknapp and his crew of juvenile idiots.' Crabbe blushed again. 'I'd like to see his drawing. I really would. They should make people show what they've done before leaving. You were sitting next to him. What was on his sheet?' She looked up at Crabbe suddenly realising her faux pas. 'He's your friend, isn't he. Isn't he? I'm such a . . . I'm sorry.'

'It doesn't matter,' said Crabbe. He took another sip of Noggin.

'You don't look like . . .' She shook her head again, censoring whatever it was she was going to say.

'I don't look like one of his friends?'

'It doesn't matter.' She was looking away from him now. He wanted to carry on the conversation. She was pretty and warm and felt clever and fun.

'I'm his accountant. Originally.'

'You're not his accountant any more?'

'I am actually. But we bonded. Over music hall.'

'I don't know him. So just ignore me.'

'I understand. What you're saying.' There was an awkward pause. 'Have you come to one of these before?' She smiled. Crabbe was pleased.

'It's why I got Russell to sign me in. Otherwise I can't come down. When Carol's not here. I love them. You can guarantee whoever it is – is going to be interesting. To draw, I mean.'

'Are you an artist?'

She laughed and shook her head. 'I'm an actor. But I love to draw.'

'You're late,' said Siobhan. She was sitting at the kitchen table. A pile of exercise books next to her.

'Meeting. Tax planning for CFC. It was the only time they could do. Wanted a drink afterwards.' He went over to the kettle and filled it.

She looked up at him, her pen suspended over the book

she was marking. 'There's some pasta in the pan. It's only pesto. Salad in the fridge.'

Crabbe sat in front of the telly in the living room – not watching a repeat of *Frasier*. Siobhan had gone to bed, tired. He found himself thinking about Davina. He put his nose in the sleeve of his jumper and got a hit of her perfume, felt it in the base of his stomach. He pulled his head up sharply, realising what he'd done.

Crabbe avoided the Challenge Club for the next week, despite the guilt this brought him at having spent the money on membership. He had planned to tell Siobhan, how necessary it was for his work, how many of his clients were members and that it was useful to be able to arrange meetings there – given what unconventional hours most of them worked. And these all sounded like legitimate concerns. The fee was tax-deductible. Why did he feel the need to be so covert about it? He kept away for another week, and then a call from Tommy Redknapp prompted him to attend again.

'Crabcake. Thought you'd like this one. Didn't think you'd want to miss it.' It was a games night. Old board games from the sixties and seventies, but perfect examples of them – in some cases so pristine that just to handle the pieces was like slipping back in time. They were sitting in front of Railroader, a Waddingtons game that recreated the advance of the railways across the United States in the middle of the nineteenth century. Little interlocking pieces of plastic track ran across the board.

Crabbe still felt uncomfortable in the dinner suit. It's possible his discomfort was added to by the deception involved – he had to keep it in his office, get changed into it at the end of the day, and take a replacement jacket in his bag together with a tie, which he put on in the taxi home. The black trousers weren't actually those of his dinner suit, they were more anonymous, all-purpose suit trousers, so they'd provoke no suspicion folded on the back of his chair in the bedroom.

'My uncle had this, you know,' said Crabbe, 'I remember laying the bits of track out. I never played the game.'

'Story of your life, Crabcake.'

'I'm playing now, aren't I,' he said trying not to sound defensive.

'Yeah, you're playing now. Shake that dice, man.' Laughter around the table.

In truth Crabbe was still in his trial period. A portion of the fee had been paid, but he was entitled to come to the club for three months. If he liked them – and more importantly perhaps if they liked him – at the end of that time full membership would be activated. He was trying not to work too hard at it, trying to be casual in his approach, not to seem needy – this, he told himself, was the reason for holding off going for a couple of weeks rather than being down there every night. It was the same strategy he had used to woo some big clients, and indeed the one he had learned to employ when wooing Siobhan. Despite this intention, however, now he had a scent of what it was like, Crabbe was unable – or found it intolerable – to miss any of the proceedings, particularly the occasions that seemed to have been made for him, opportunities for him finally to display his deepest enthusiasms. Maybe he deserved to be part of this glittering world after all.

The games evening ran as a tournament. One progressed from Railroader to Game of Life, to the more difficult, adult games – Risk, Democracy, Kingmaker. These took longer, they could go on for several hours. One could of course leave, but to Crabbe this would display a lack of commitment – the kind of thing the club would be looking out for when making its final decision about whether to grant full membership. It was the opposite situation to the 'playing it cool' strategy. One had to know the difference in life and when to employ which mode. The more nights he attended, the more he saw how important it was to his career that he conduct himself well throughout this period. To be admitted into these higher circles, to be accepted and seen as being on a par with these people, who were increasingly his sole client base, the more likely he was to flourish. In addition he had a talent for the strategy games that made up the latter part of the competition. He was even confident about the possibility of winning.

He found himself sitting opposite Davina Skinner for the final game. It was called North Sea Oil and it dated from 1978. The pieces were cheap – thin cardboard playing surface, paper money, bright plastic counters like upturned nipples – but the game itself was unexpectedly cunning. You had to bid for drilling rights, buy equipment and then sell your oil – though of course there were many other factors to take into account, things that it was easy to assume were of no moment whatsoever. A change in government perhaps, differing motives and agendas around the board depending upon the position of the player's rigs, even the weather – all of these could feed in to the eventual outcome of each round. In order to complete the game within the allotted time knockout rules applied. After thirty minutes Davina and Crabbe were the only remaining players. Crabbe had to make a decision – was he going to sell Hewett and Dotty in order to drill down speculatively in a region to the north of Viking or was he going to hold firm to his initial strategy of accumulating as many barrels as he could? Davina's doll-like, rounded face gave away nothing of her intentions. In the end Crabbe decided to take a risk – it was uncharacteristic perhaps, but increasingly he found it was something he was prepared to do. Three more rigs came his way – Indefatigable, Ann and Amethyst. He won the game – and the tournament.

'You're a skilful player,' said Davina afterwards, pushing her hand through hair that seemed to shimmer in the coloured lights of Tony Wilson (the top-floor bar where the tournament had taken place).

'But you were unlucky,' said Crabbe. He felt a confidence, a swagger, that was quite unfamiliar. There was a thrill about it. Had he been this person always, concealed from himself by the enervating shadow his family cast within?

'Luck doesn't come into it,' she said sipping at the vodka and cranberry juice which seemed quite black in the blue glare of the bar.

It was a hot Sunday afternoon – early June but it felt like August – the air dry and searing in the tiny brick-walled yard at the back of Crabbe and Siobhan's house. They sat in sun-loungers – a pair they had bought in the auction house on Essex Road two years before. It was rare for these to come out of the shed, but here they were, unfolded and horizontal beneath the north London sky. Crabbe had one finger inserted between the thin plastic tubing and the stretched canvas it bound to the aluminium frame around it. He pulled and twisted, momentarily enjoying the sensation of tension the tube afforded. Then it began to hurt and he struggled to disengage his digit. It came out sharply scraping the knuckle against a rough piece of metal. He held it up to his face to examine it. There was a tiny dot of blood livid on the skin. Siobhan lay next to him, eyes half closed, the *Observer* spread over her chest. Her thighs were squashed against the dark-blue fabric of the recliner. They looked unexpectedly thick and fat, like his grandmother's – an illusion he knew, caused by an unfortunate conjunction of her shorts, the chair and her position in it – but he found he had to look away because he was fleetingly revolted. The sun hurt his eyes so he closed them. He saw redness, the lines of capillaries. This too was uncomfortable. He squeezed his eyes tighter to obliterate the image.

Young again – alone in school – thirteen? Fourteen? A line of them together at the back of the class. Andy Dale, who built radios for fun and could be heard talking to himself in the corridors, mouthing streams of numbers and letters – perhaps types of capacitors and triodes, perhaps just random nonsense. Desmond Hurwicz – 'Dessy Dezzer'. Everyone thought Desmond was a derogatory nickname. Crabbe knew otherwise. It was in fact Hurwicz's real name. This had been confessed to Crabbe one Thursday afternoon as if it were a sin – sat at the side of the side of the water in the chlorinated cavern of the swimming pool, both of them excused with colds. And Richard Price – whose syllables all disintegrated into an amorphous mush when he spoke owing to a cleft pallet. He, Crabbe, didn't belong there – cast out with these Ishmaels near the cupboard full of damaged text books. He had never found his place. Was there no place for him to find?

But there was another memory, long ago – before this – from a time when he had been acceptable, he'd had friends. He'd felt clever – he was known for his chattiness, his enthusiasm, his love of jokes and joking. He was leaving Shipton Heath primary school to go to prep school – his parents' aspirations for him had begun young – he could only have been seven. His teacher at Shipton, Mrs Lind, was a warm, pretty girl with a foreign accent, though she spoke English perfectly. She had always liked him – encouraged his funny stories, praised the book of cartoons he had done in art. She behaved towards him as if he were special, not in a way that detracted from anybody else, but just as if that were who he was. The only cloud in this sunny relationship had appeared at the school bonfire. Crabbe had been talking to her in his voluble way – about Blackpool and fossils and Miss World and his uncle's boardgame Boobytrap which hurt your fingers if you lost. She was there with her husband – a big, confident, long-haired man who looked like the hero in a Friday night television series. At one point as Crabbe had been talking to Mrs Lind, enjoying being with her and entertaining her and being special, he had seen the husband catch her eye and open and close his fingers rapidly. Crabbe understood the gesture and the criticism it implied. In that moment he was a silly, stupid child who spoke too much. He wasn't special at all.

But this incident aside, his relationship with the beautiful Mrs Lind continued and on his last week at school, in a moment of uncharacteristic boldness, he asked if he could do a show – to say goodbye to his fellow pupils and perhaps most importantly to Mrs Lind. In truth Crabbe didn't know what this show would be – just that he wanted to give it. He supposed he was going to stand up and do jokes, tell stories. It would come to him. The day of the performance arrived. Crabbe found himself at the front of the class. He could not now remember the events before this, the build-up to it, whether he had felt nervous or excited. But what was vivid was the memory of standing there, before the class, grasping the side of the wooden table behind him, its splintered edge. A moment in which shame engulfed him like the blackest of clouds – a swelling horror that he had nothing to say to his classmates, nothing prepared to entertain them with, no jokes or stories. He didn't in fact know how to. There was an abyss, an emptiness, filled only with his own stupid aspiration and its hollow consequence. Like a dream from which he couldn't awake he became imprisoned in that moment – having to mouth inanities, random words, anything to fill the terrible, terrible silence he found himself alone with though in the presence of his peers. Finally Mrs Lind had intervened. She clapped, bringing Crabbe's evident discomfort to an end. Although his time at Shipton Heath had ended shortly after that his memory of Mrs Lind and her kindness to him was forever tainted by this abortive performance and how he must have let her down.

Siobhan was holding his hand, her arm resting lightly on the side of her sun-lounger. He opened his eyes to see a plane roaring low overhead, crawling slowly and fixedly across the bright-blue sky, as if on a rail.

The next games night had a different feel. Not board-games, but parlour games. At first Crabbe was disappointed but then, when the nature of the games they were to play was revealed, he became more cheerful. The first one was a simple warm-up – a bout of wink murder. He'd enjoyed this at parties as a child. Every aspect of it yielded pleasure – the mystery and puzzle of who was the murderer and who the detective, the tension of whether you would be a victim, the opportunity to act out your own death, as extravagantly as you chose. Playing it now, in a darkened fire-lit drawing room in a perfect simulation of Victorian London, Crabbe was transported back to the intensity of the pleasure he had known as a child. Plus there was the added guilt-tinged delight of seeing Davina standing in the circle opposite him, the bright sheen of her lipstick almost black in the flickering dimness. Being an actress, her death, when it came, was something of note. It was delicate, beautiful, shocking, arousing and stirring. The guttural cry she gave out resolved into a series of gentle gurgles, almost like whimpers. Her right foot twitched and spasmed. Her little red shoe fell off. Crabbe was jarred by her skill. He couldn't help but stare at her, curled on the floor, seemingly lifeless. When he looked up again Tommy Redknapp was winking at him. It took him a moment to remember that this meant he'd been murdered.

There was a break for tea halfway through the evening. A thin, Russian-looking man, crisp white apron tied neatly around the black clothes beneath, pushed in a chrome urn on a custom-built trolley. He passed round cups of Assam on small plates that contained biscuits, a thimble-sized tumbler of milk and a rock of white sugar. The biscuits were hand-baked. A discussion had started as to what was the worst movie ever made. An air of enthusiastic bonhomie. The comedian Simon Onions shaking his head, crying with laughter, trying to get his words out.

'Have you ever seen *Bullseye?*'

'*Bullseye?*' said Tommy Redknapp.

Crabbe felt himself laughing already, even though nothing funny had been said.

'This film,' said Simon Onions. 'This film is the worst film you have ever seen. I don't just mean bad or boring or non-sensical. Technically it is so inept that you cannot believe it has been wrought by professional men.'

Crabbe looked across at Davina. She was smiling too – a broad, clever, arch smile. She looked to her left, at him. Normally he would have looked away. He didn't. And she didn't either.

Simon Onions continued his critique. 'Let's begin with Michael Caine's accent. His attempt at an American accent. The sheer poverty of it . . .' A rush of feeling overcame Crabbe. There was Davina looking at him, smiling. Here he was in the company of clever, funny, talented individuals – maybe some of the smartest people in the country. And they were nice. They were warm. They were welcoming. And here he was with them. He was here with them.

Davina walked down with Crabbe to the cloakroom in the basement. Crabbe withdrew his new overcoat. It was dark blue, cashmere. He'd bought it in the sale at Harvey Nichols. Told Siobhan how important it was for the clients to see him looking not unlike they did.

'Nice coat,' said Davina.

'It feels nice on,' said Crabbe, wincing as he spoke. There was nothing clever about that.

'Have you got my number?' she said, rummaging in her handbag.

'Sorry?'

'My number, did I give you my number?'

'Erm . . .'

'If you're coming down – you can text. It's nice to know if other people are going to be there.' She looked up at him. Crabbe hoped he wasn't blushing. 'Or I could text you . . .' she added.

'I've never done this before.' The words were banal. What they said didn't need saying. But Crabbe said them anyway.

'I have,' said Davina. 'Once.'

'Who was it?' He immediately regretted asking the question.

'You don't want to know.' An awkward pause. 'It was . . . I regret it now. I was younger. Stupider. I was angry with Carol. He'd been up to his old tricks. It was just some man. Not a man. A boy. I let him pick me up.'

'So what's this?' Crabbe's mouth was dry. More banalities. His heart thudding away like he was in the queue for a roller-coaster.

'I don't know,' said Davina after a moment.

'Are you angry with him now? Is it another one of those?' Crabbe felt like an idiot for asking the question. Every word he spoke felt gauche and unworldly.

'Never mind me,' said Davina. 'Why are you giving me the third degree? What about you? Have you ever done it before? This, I mean.' She seemed as uncomfortable as him. She folded her legs up underneath her, settling herself on the unusually firm hotel bed. She pulled her skirt around them with what seemed – given where they were and what they were about to do – surprising modesty. It was typical of the kind of contradictory behaviour that had drawn him to her. Crabbe breathed in slowly, thought about her question. He felt close to her in the moment and wanted to answer it coherently.

'No.' Another long pause. The noise of traffic outside. Gower Street. Central London. The world of people and their daily business. He was no different from any one of them. No better. But no worse. 'I don't suppose I know what I'm doing either.' He laughed. 'When I was fourteen . . .' He paused.

'Go on,' she said.

'When I was fourteen I broke the kettle. At home. I don't know why. I did it deliberately. Took a screwdriver to it inside and pulled the element out of its socket. I couldn't tell you why.'

'Is that was this is, then? A piece of senseless nihilism. Doesn't sound very romantic.'

'I don't know you, Davina,' Crabbe heard himself saying. 'I think you're very beautiful.' That was true. He did. 'This whole . . . the club. That world. Siobhan doesn't approve of any of it.' He wished he hadn't used her name. For a moment preceding it he had felt like he was in a neutral space where this liaison was acceptable – or at least permissible. 'What I'm trying to . . . What I want to say is that it . . . this . . . the club . . . it feels like me. For the first time. Like a me I've wanted to be. And you . . . you're part of that.'

'I'm part of that? Part of the new you?'

'Does that sound selfish? Just about me?'

'Tell me more about the new you. What does it want to do? What is it?'

Crabbe thought for a minute. He looked into her eyes. She stared back, urging him to talk, wanting him to talk. 'It's . . . free. And whole. And finally . . . finally . . . finally . . . being . . . being . . .' He could feel a great weight opposing the words. He was determined to use all of his willpower to push against it. '. . . Being me. Finally being me.' He felt tears in the corners of his eyes. The release of it. The hope. That somehow this was the beginning of the fulfilment he had been yearning for all his life, since he had been conscious of anticipating a future. It might be a messy and awkward beginning but that description could apply to most births. He reached for Davina. He was surprised when he sensed her withdraw.

'What is it?' he said – suddenly feeling alarmed.

'Nothing,' said Davina. 'Why not keep talking.'

'I thought . . .' His voice trailed off. He waited for her to say something, some explanation. He reached for her again. She flinched. There was a noise from the wardrobe. Something hidden shifting. Crabbe turned his head. It must have come from next door. But then it was followed by a giggle, which sounded much closer.

'What was that?' said Crabbe, alert.

'What?' said Davina.

'That noise.'

'I didn't hear anything.'

Another noise now, like speech. Something muffled. 'That. That!' Crabbe banged the bed. He looked at Davina – waited for her to respond in some way. She looked at him blankly. Crabbe felt anger swelling within him – an irrational anger – a temper. He suddenly wanted to hit her without knowing way. He hadn't realised that his emotions were capable of such volatility. He thought she would get up off the bed, go and investigate for herself. She didn't. She remained there inert, unmoving, seemingly frozen. Crabbe jumped up, still feeling the burning anger. His movements were angular, jerky. He reached the sliding wardrobe in one stride and threw the door open. It made a grinding noise as it rolled like a millstone across its track. Inside the wardrobe were a number of people – perhaps six or seven – several BAFTA award-winners among them. In the middle, stifling his trademark giggle, was Tommy Redknapp. They were holding bottles – beer, wine – one of them swigged from a clear plastic glass, the kind you normally bought smoothies in. They were all drunk.

'Room for one more inside,' said Tommy. Someone else spoke though Crabbe couldn't see who. Perhaps it was Simon Onions.

'Oh God. Not him, though,' it said. 'We don't want *him* in here.' More laughter. 'Finally ... finally ... finally,' said a second voice perfectly imitating Crabbe's Cheshire burr. Unrestrained hilarity at this. '... Being me.' The voice started singing: 'I gotta be me, I gotta be me. What else can I be but what I am.' Tommy Redknapp, tears of laughter in his scrunched-up eyes, tapped out a rhythmic flourish on the wire coathangers that surrounded him – bum badda dum bum. Crabbe turned to find Davina but she was already gone – perhaps hiding in the tiny bathroom.

'It was just a lark, mate – just having some fun.' Tommy was trotting after Crabbe as he marched down the seemingly endless hotel corridor. Crabbe just needed to get out of there – into the light, into the sun. He needed to drink something. Maybe he would find a pub – a dark small pub and sit in the corner. He needed to think. He could feel Tommy behind him, regulating his pace so as not to catch up. 'It was just a dare. Just a joke.' Crabbe felt white inside. There was rage but it wouldn't come out. The shame was bigger. He felt all the hate but compliance was still more important. (How could it be more important? How could he be so naive, so stupid? How could he have got himself into that position? Leave it. Leave it. Leave it.) 'Mate . . .' Crabbe strode on. Tommy's voice diminished.

He found the pub – small, dark and anonymous – a few streets from Russell Square. Had he witnessed a murder while there Crabbe wouldn't have been able to tell anybody a thing about it. He held a tall glass full of ice and Southern Comfort under his nose – let the fumes sit in his nostrils. She hadn't wanted him. She'd had no interest in him. It was a trick or a joke or a dare. And him? He was never going to be made a member. Of course not. It wasn't possible. He didn't have the requisite stuff to be in that club. He never would. He never could. He wasn't funny enough, clever enough, sharp-witted enough, gifted enough, interesting enough, talented enough. Good enough. He would never be good enough. Could never be good enough. It made him feel sick that he was even presumptuous enough to have considered it, to have dared to stand up there on that platform, to have promoted himself. He swigged down the last of his drink, let the ice touch his lip, where it burned.

Thankfully Siobhan was already sleeping when he got home, drunk, sick, hurting. He was angry now, enough alcohol to set these thoughts free. Siobhan lay pooled on the sofa, asleep with the television on. Tommy Redknapp and Carol Skinner on *QI*. He wanted to kick the screen. He hated it. He went upstairs and sat on the toilet. He didn't know what to do. Was there anything to be done? He stared at Siobhan's pants on the radiator – three pairs lined up. One lacy, two plain, though there was nothing frumpy about the plain. He thought of Davina's pants, which he never got to see. He thought about the fact that he'd wanted to. Had been excited about seeing her naked. He thought about what he had wanted to do with her. Thought about how he could have done this to Siobhan. He slid off the toilet, feeling himself contract, twisted round, banged his chin on the porcelain and vomited, hearing its resonant splash reverberate around the pan, which made him heave again. And again.

When he got into bed Siobhan was already there, though once again he was grateful she was asleep. He got in as quietly as he could. He'd considered sleeping on the spare bed but was terrified cold at the thought of what this might communicate to her. His shame continued to swell. He tried to sleep. He felt a chill despite the duvet rolled around him. And then his phone chirruped loudly. He had a text message. The mobile was in his trousers on the chair. It was ten past one. Who would be texting now? With surprising speed he rolled out of the bed and dug in the pile of clothes until he'd located the phone. His heart racing before he'd even seen it. It was from Davina. 'I'm sorry. Please call. Dx'. He rushed to erase it before Siobhan could stir. Even as he inserted the phone back among the clothing it buzzed again. 'I mean it. I really mean it. Please Justin. Dx'. He deleted it again.

And so Crabbe found himself, against everything he knew was right or decent, or just, waiting in the bar of the Royal Festival Hall – near Waterloo and his practice – for Davina. He felt sick. And even more attracted to her than he had done before the sorry discovery of the previous night. There she was, tiny by the double doors – a plain grey coat, over grey trouser suit. Was there an attempt to demonstrate contrition in the tenor of her outfit? He watched her for a moment, to see what she would do, as one animal might watch another, trying to determine whether it is prey or predator. She scanned the open space, searching for him. She found him. Involuntarily Crabbe gave a little wave. He pulled his hand down sharply, not wishing to give any indication of forgiveness or acceptance. He watched her walk towards him. She smiled sadly, then looked down at the floor, keeping her eyes off him for most of her passage.

'Hello,' she said.

'Hello,' said Crabbe.

'I'm so sorry,' she said. He felt like he was seeing her for the first time. She looked different. A little less pretty, a little less perfect. He sensed her herness the same as his hisness – sitting inside her – tiny and vulnerable like the *homunculus* inside a Dalek.

'Do you want a coffee?' He heard the banality of the request hanging in the airportish air.

'Can I have some wine?'

'Red? White?'

'Can you see if they have a rosé?'

Oh, he hated that.

'It was all Tommy's idea,' she said, holding the wineglass against her chin. 'He knew how much I wanted to join. Needed to join.'

'Why did you need to join?'

'Why did you?'

'I didn't need to join.' He heard the testiness in his own voice.

'You were always there. You came to every meeting they asked you to come to. Sticking to the letter of your probation.'

'That's not true,' said Crabbe. But he remembered that even the events he missed had been consciously avoided – his attempt to conceal his own desperation. He sipped at his coffee, felt the bite of it on his tongue. If this was about anything wasn't it letting the *homunculus* out of the Dalek. He put down the coffee cup. She looked at his face then looked down at her Fendi handbag, fiddling with the clasp.

'I'm getting a divorce,' she said. Crabbe felt himself tighten.

'What?' he heard himself say.

'Not because of . . . Not . . .' She was blushing. She started again. 'I decided last night,' she said. 'I walked round the house – up and down the stairs – looking at all the things. Carol rang and left a message. It was a funny message. It made me laugh. I didn't want to laugh. I started touching all the things. It was a thing I used to do before. I'd have to do it or else I couldn't get to sleep. I thought, I'm not having this again. Something's got to change. Something radical.' She looked up at him, her eyes wet, the corners blackening as the make-up began to run. He thought about her skill as an actress.

'Why did you do it – why were we in that hotel room?'

'They were going to let me join. Be the first woman member. If I could . . . If I . . .' she came to a halt.

'What were you supposed to do?'

'Make someone fall for me,' she said. Now the room was cold. A fridge on a hot day. 'Someone . . . unlikely.' And now it was a freezer. His heart was racing again. Fury. Fury was the word. Furious. A hurricane in a bottle. An earthquake in a pebble. He got up. The stool fell over behind him. He knew what she was telling him already – a priori. Why was he angry again?

'You . . . stupid.' Through the eye of a needle. 'Little . . .' Out came the camel. 'Cunt.' He kicked the stool hard. It hurt his foot. He marched off across the expensive carpet.

She found him sitting outside on the South Bank – on a bench near the National Film Theatre.

'I've hurt you,' she said. He wouldn't look at her. 'I've hurt you. And I'm sorry. I'm sorry.' The rage had not abated for Crabbe. The brutal lines of the surrounding architecture were made fluid by the tears in his eyes. Thirty-seven years old. Crying in public. 'It's me all over,' said Davina. 'I shouldn't be allowed out in the world. I can't help it. I—' Something about the third 'I' in a row sprang the mechanism. Just like Boobytrap, his uncle's game from all those years ago. Pull out the wrong piece and – wham! He set upon her. That was the only description. Crabbe set upon her. Part of him described the action to himself as he did it. He pummelled her with his balled fists. She was tiny beneath him – like a hamster. He could feel her ribs. She screamed out. Little yelps at first, then bigger. Great whoops of air. He thought he might have been screaming too. It was like coming.

The police had arrived very quickly. They must have been on the beat nearby. And it was Siobhan who came to collect him from the cells at Agar Street police station. He wasn't going to tell her anything. By midnight he had told her everything. He found he was on his knees, in the small living room – the curtains still open he had been talking for so long. Her tears burned him more than his own.

Davina was bruised, not injured. She didn't press charges and neither did the CPS. Crabbe had felt sure he would lose his practice. And his wife.

It was Siobhan's idea and it came almost a year to the day after his confession. For three months things had not been good. There was much silence around the house. And an amount of time spent apart. For a period Crabbe had thought about leaving and renting a studio flat in town – not because he wanted to be apart from Siobhan – he didn't – she felt like the only thing of any value in his life. Rather because he wanted to be away from the pain and the difficulty and the anxiety. He went as far as finding out how much it would cost. But he decided to stay in the house and endure the feelings – which, he acknowledged, were a simple consequence of his own actions. But there they were, the following July, sitting in the small garden, enjoying the gentle warmth of a perfectly sunny day.

'You should start your own club.'

'What?' he said.

'You should start your own club. But anyone can join.'

'Anyone can join?'

'Anyone can join.' She was sitting upright in her lounger smiling, one leg curled underneath herself.

And so the first meeting of the Ishmael Club took place on Highbury Fields, Saturday 8 August. Crabbe, Siobhan, Siobhan's brother, her two nephews and three of Crabbe's clients convened on the field closest to Highbury Corner, meeting near the back of the children's playground. After sharing croissants and coffee from a flask they began a game of rounders. Crabbe hadn't played rounders since he was at Shipton Heath – but it was the last time he remembered enjoying a sport. Back then there had been no selecting of teams and no anxiety about performance. You just played. He thought he wouldn't still know the rules – but he did. Racing round the grass, the smell of damp turf, feeling pleasantly thirsty from the exertion, knowing there were cold drinks in Siobhan's big bag of food, Crabbe experienced a rush of simple happiness and let it pass. Afterwards, sitting beneath a big horse chestnut tree, he talked to Siobhan's youngest nephew Adam, who was saving up to go to Borneo to help orang-utans. He looked across and saw his clients laughing, leaning back relaxed, their arms stretched out behind them. At the end of the meeting everyone sat in a circle and talked about what kind of other things they might like to do. The issue of membership was simple. If the subject ever came up with anyone, should they ask about it, they could join. Anyone who asked to join, could. The only criteria that needed to be fulfilled was the desire to join. Desire it, and you were a member.

Without quite knowing how it came about, Crabbe found that after four months the Ishmael Club had over seven hundred members, and it was growing all the time. There were no official premises, though occasionally halls were hired, depending on the event. Dances, gigs, film shows, magic shows. The necessary licences were dealt with by going to the appropriately licensed premises on a case by case basis. It was very simple. And very cheap.

The best thing? For Crabbe the best thing was the conversation. He found something he hadn't known since he was seven years old. It was possible to talk to anybody, and for them to talk to you too. Making this discovery was, without any doubt, the single most exciting thing Crabbe had ever done in his life.

Out of Bounds

Lower Fellstow hadn't always been a school. Indeed Bolling, the headmaster's son, took great delight in excavating its true heritage whenever he could.

It was the end of Michaelmas term and everyone – boys and staff – had left, save the aforementioned Bolling and two more: Bolling's best friend Luke Avenall and an overweight, red-faced fourth-former named, unfortunately for him, Lavabo. Neither Avenall or Bolling knew Lavabo's first name. In truth they barely knew him at all. He was a great fat inconvenience and he was only there because his mother was unable to pick him up until the following day. Bolling and Luke had been looking forward to their own private adventures. The headmaster and his wife were taking their annual shopping trip to Leeds and staying over with a cousin in Roundhay, and that meant the boys had the school entirely to themselves.

How to describe Lower Fellstow? A 'great neo-gothic monstrosity', said Nicholas Pevsner on a visit to the private chapel that lay in the overgrown grounds. It was not a beautiful building, but to a boy with any imagination it was a palace of thrills. Even on a fine day it stood gloomy against the sky, its elaborate castellations and leering gargoyles somewhat at odds with the bleakness of the surrounding moorland. The building was even stranger when one knew a little of its heritage, as Bolling was about to explain.

'Come on, Loverboy, keep up.'

'Can't we watch the telly?'

'We're exploring.'

'But I don't want to. I don't feel well.' Lavabo wheezed unconvincingly.

'He doesn't have to come,' said Luke.

'You can wait in the flat if you want, Loverboy, but the leccy's on a meter. It'll probably run out, and I'm the one with all the 50ps. You'd have to sit in the dark till we came back and that might be one or two in the morning. It's up to you.' Bolling looked at Lavabo as if he were giving him a fair choice. Lavabo pushed at one side of his glasses.

'Why can't we have the lights on?' This from Luke, who thought it might help with Lavabo's nerves.

'Because Dad's turned the school mains off, and I'm in charge.'

They continued walking, following Bolling's bobbing torchlight as it picked out details ahead of them. Things that were part of the mundanity of their everyday school life took on a different, more sinister air. A bronze reproduction of the Hever Castle Pan cast a huge shadow which crept across the cream painted wall as they moved past. Lavabo gasped audibly when they rounded the next corner.

'It's only Basil,' said Bolling, yawning.

The tatty stuffed fox that resided in a glass case above the sick bay wouldn't normally merit a second glance, even from Lavabo. Viewed now it seemed a different object entirely. Its glass eyes glinted in the torchlight, the shifting reflection animating them momentarily.

'But where are we going?' Lavabo was making more of an effort to keep up with them. It hadn't been dark when they left the top-floor apartment. Now the sky beyond the windows was quite black. Bolling didn't answer Lavabo's question, he just turned and smiled, swinging the torch beam upwards, holding it under his own face. They passed through a curtained alcove and walked a short distance down the low-ceilinged arched corridor beyond it, coming to rest in front of a broad white door. 'We can't go down here. You know we can't go down here,' said Lavabo, panicked. 'The cellar's out of bounds.'

'In school hours. In term time,' said Bolling grinning.

'I want to go back. It's not safe.'

'You're with me.'

'Sir – I mean your . . .' He hesitated a moment before starting up again. 'Your . . . father said – it's not safe.'

'They've dug out a pit. That's all. We know where it is. I just want to show you something.'

'*Is* it safe?' said Luke in a low voice. In truth had it just been the two of them he most likely wouldn't have asked the question.

'Are you chickening out now?'

'Maybe we should just go back.'

'You're with me.' Bolling began to twist the key in its lock.

'I don't want to,' said Lavabo suddenly.

'We're going down.'

'I don't want to,' said Lavabo again, holding on to his glasses and shifting slightly from one foot to the other.

'In case you didn't realise, I'm in charge here,' said Bolling.

'I'm not going down there. It's not safe. They've been digging.'

'You going to stay up here? On your own?' Bolling smiled dubiously. Lavabo stared at him.

'Yes.'

'Let him stay here,' said Luke. He saw Lavabo's fear. Felt sorry for him in the moment. Remembered something about him losing his father in the summer holidays.

'I'll give him a choice,' said Bolling. He can either go into the grounds, on his own, into the woods, down to the holly-bushes near the beck – where it's darkest – pick some holly to prove he's been and bring it back.' Lavabo looked at him, blinking. 'Or we go down in the cellar.' Lavabo carried on staring. His eyes were wide behind his glasses. Luke shivered. A draught blew down the narrow corridor. There was a grimy skylight above them. Outside, above, was featureless blackness. 'Too scared to do it? A scaredy weredy cat?'

'I'm not,' said Lavabo. Luke sensed tears not far behind. 'I'm not scared.'

Bolling reached into his back pocket, held out the torch. Lavabo just looked at them.

'No? Don't want to? Well, come on, then. Let's get on with it.' He reached out and twisted the heavy old key in its lock.

The stairs into the cellar were treacherous enough. The stone was chipped, chunks missing in places. The levels between steps were irregular. The boys bunched together as they descended, focusing on Bolling's flickering torch beam. The air was damp and cold.

'They have been digging? Haven't they?' said Luke, keeping his eyes fixed on the descent.

'Looking for bodies,' said Bolling, turning briefly to look at Lavabo. 'Corpses.'

'Drains,' said Luke trying to keep the fat boy calm. 'They're repairing the drains.'

They came down into the cellar proper. An open area with a sandy floor and various disused items of school furniture. Lavabo jumped as something crunched under foot.

'Careful,' shouted Bolling his voice dulled by the enclosed space. A flash of torch beam revealed broken glass – the remains of an old aquarium. Lavabo pulled his foot back. The torch swung upwards revealing a huge dark expanse ahead. The light flickered for a moment as if it was about to die, the darkness threatening to take them. Bolling shook the torch. The beam strengthened. Luke took in the unexpected scale of the space.

'It's so big.'

Bolling looked at Luke, then tapped his nose.

'You know Lower Fellstow wasn't always a school?' Luke shrugged his shoulders. 'Did you know that, Loverboy? That

Lower Fellstow wasn't always a school?' No reply from Lavabo. 'It used to be a gaming house,' said Bolling, a hint of pride in his voice.

'What's a gaming house?'

'You know who Daniel Lancaster was, Loverboy?'

'Beer,' came the sullen response.

'Beer. Top marks. A brewer needed a country seat. Somewhere he could throw a party.'

The ground became more uneven as they progressed; walls of shelves, stacked with upended chairs, gave way to bare brick, some of it covered in places with a doughy white mould. After a while they came to a halt. Bolling lifted his torch up to the low, light-coloured ceiling. The small halo of light was crowded with black lines and marks.

'What are they?' Luke peered up at them. There were names. Dates. Lavabo read aloud: 'Diane Savage 1923. Christopher Lax 4.4.1927. Oudolf 1929.'

'How are they written there? It's not ink.' Luke was standing on his toes peering at the markings.

'Candles,' said Bolling. 'They're burned in.' Lavabo reached up to touch them.

'What's that?' Lavabo seemed to have momentarily lost his fear. He was intrigued by a shape at the end of one of the names. Something like a triangle, pointing downward. It had two lines in its top two corners. Bolling shrugged. 'It looks like an animal,' said Lavabo, slightly puzzled. Bolling swept his torch beam along the rest of the ceiling. A chaotic mess of more names seemed to fill every inch. Most of them were accompanied by a similar symbol.

'What were they doing down here?' said Luke.

'Can't we go back now?' Lavabo was looking nervously over his shoulder. 'I'm cold.' As if to confirm this he exhaled noisily, creating a cloud of breath which hung in the torchlight.

'Just a bit further.' Bolling walked on.

They came to a kind of junction. On one side was an irregular archway – visible through it were piled-up earth and excavations. On the other side was an empty doorframe. It looked like it used to carry an array of bolts and locks. There were strikes and mortise holes all down one side. The door, however, had been removed. 'This way,' said Bolling confidently.

'What if we get lost?' said Lavabo. Luke could hear the fear rising in the fat boy's speech.

'We won't.' Bolling's torch ranged around the chamber. The reach of the torchlight fell off before it found a wall. It faded out into darkness and damp, chilly space.

'What did they do down here?' said Luke, repeating his earlier question.

'Let's add our names.' Bolling had placed the torch on a brick. He was digging out a faded box of candles half buried in the sandy floor.

'No!' said Lavabo, almost shouting, his voice seemingly deadened by the thick darkness barely kept at bay by the torch. But Bolling had already lit a candle, using a lighter he pulled from his blazer pocket. The guttering flame revealed more of the low ceiling. There were no names burned here. Just versions of the shape, the strange triangular shape that accompanied the earlier graffiti. The shapes were inscribed in differing sizes. One of the designs – the largest in size – had curling coiled ears and pinprick eyes. 'We might start a fire,' said Lavabo, fearful.

'You go first,' said Bolling.

'No,' said Lavabo. But he took the candle as Bolling handed it to him.

'Go on, Loverboy.'

Luke had picked up the torch. He ranged it around the space, maybe trying to find the far wall. There was no sign of it. Only distant, receding blackness. He illuminated a pile of earth. Next to it was a large pit. It looked less like a workman had made it – more like something dug by an animal. When he looked back he saw Lavabo carefully completing his name in soot. To Luke's surprise the boy had drawn his own miniature version of the triangular head. It looked like an insect. Bolling added his, and then it was Luke's turn. Bolling took the torch off him. Luke held the candle, raising it to the ceiling, burning his name in black, inch by careful inch. For some reason he was reluctant to add a shape and was going to avoid doing so, until, upon seeing Bolling's design, he changed his mind. He completed the apex of his triangle and blew out the candle. The shimmering shape of the chamber solidified a little around them.

'When did it become a school?' said Luke.

'The place was abandoned. Then it was requisitioned. During the war. Lancaster had been arrested. He was a fascist. A collaborator.' This said with some glee. 'It became a school after.'

'Why did they abandon it?' At that moment everything went black. Luke heard something which he assumed to be Lavabo. A sharp whimper as if the boy had been physically struck. 'What is it? What's happened?'

'Torch. Shit. Shit!' said Bolling audibly shaking the torch. Luke thought about the hole. The open pit somewhere behind them. They mustn't lose their sense of direction.

'Stand still. Just stand still.'

'I want to get out,' said Lavabo. Luke had never experienced blackness like this. A total absence of light.

'I don't remember where the door is. Do you remember where the door is?' Bolling sounded like he too was suppressing panic.

'Stop it. Stop it, Bolling. I want to get out.'

'Shit. I don't know what . . . shit.' Luke could hear Lavabo crying now. Real tears in the darkness.

'Mummy,' the fat boy said. There was a pure quality to his fear. 'I want Mummy. Please. Mummy.' On the third 'Mummy' the torch flicked back on. Bolling aimed it at Lavabo.

'Only joking,' said Bolling. He flicked it on and off, on and off, and laughed as Lavabo's pudgy wet-cheeked face strobed in and out of the darkness.

Bolling unscrewed the top of a bottle of Advocaat. Thick yellow liquid glugged out into tall fluted glasses he'd arranged on the table.

'Banana wine, Loverboy?' He handed a glass to Lavabo, who was sitting on the chair staring into the gas fire. Luke was looking round the private apartment at the top of the school.

'Doesn't it get a bit cramped? You living in here.' He picked at some of the cold meats that Mrs Bolling had lain out before she left.

'It's cosy. Plus my room's away from theirs.' He pointed towards a curtained stairwell next to the kitchenette. 'You all right now, Loverboy? Have a good sip at that. It'll warm you up. We won't tell Mummy.' The last word delivered with a hint of mockery. Luke looked at Lavabo. The boy was all turned in on himself. Luke could see the knots. For a moment he felt what it must be like being Lavabo. No friends at school during term-time. Maybe no friends at all. Uncomfortable in his own body. Little ease to be found anywhere. It was too chilly a place to spend long imagining. Luke turned away from it, helping himself to a glass of Advocaat.

Later, lying in Bolling's boy-smelling bedroom, supposedly asleep. Bolling in his bed, Luke and Lavabo in sleeping bags on the hard floor. The room lit by the gas fire, hissing blue and yellow against the chimney breast.

'Did you like your drink?' Semi-whispered from the darkness by Bolling. It brought no response. 'Hey Loverboy. Did you like your drink? I chose it specially for you. It was yellow.' Luke could hear Lavabo breathing, heavy and laboured. 'We can have something nice for breakfast, if you like? Open a tin of custard. Cowardy custard.' At this Luke felt himself laugh involuntarily. The crudeness of it. The childishness. No response from the fat boy, maybe a slight shift in his bag, in the rhythm of his breathing.

'We could have sandwiches,' said Luke. Maybe he was a little tipsy still from the drink. 'Chicken sandwiches.' Bolling laughed out loud at this. And there was a response from Lavabo. Something like a high groan or a whimper. Maybe he hadn't expected this from Luke. Avenall himself tasted something – simultaneously unpleasant and enticing. Encouraged by Bolling's laughter, he added: 'Or watch a horror film. There's something good on.'

'What is it?' asked Bolling. They were now a double act.

'The Mummy.' This bought paroxysms of laughter from them both. Silence from Lavabo. Only his breathing betrayed emotion, rapid and shorter, something injured in the darkness.

Later, much later, Luke awoke. He was thirsty, his throat and mouth dry. He stood up, shaking himself out of his sleeping bag, trying to remember if there was a sink in Bolling's room. He didn't want to have to go downstairs. In the flickering glow of the gas fire he could see that Lavabo's sleeping bag was empty. He looked around the small room. There was nowhere to hide in here. Maybe he'd got thirsty too.

Luke padded down into the flat, looked around. No Lavabo. But a note on a piece of torn foolscap written in thick charcoal pencil. 'I am not a coward', it said simply.

'Why is there only one torch?' said Luke.

'The others are locked up. You take the torch.'

'What about you?' In answer Bolling produced the lighter from his back pocket.

'He'll be all right, you know.'

Luke thought about the earthworks in the cellar. About the pit, somehow blacker against the surrounding blackness. He wondered how deep it was.

'I'll do the cellar,' said Luke. 'You do up here.'

*

The torch flickered as he reached the bottom of the uneven steps. Instinctively he kept its beam away from the ash-inscribed names on the ceiling. For some reason he didn't want to see them.

'Lavabo.' Luke's shout was immediately smothered by the thick air. He called out again. 'Lavabo!' He wished he knew the boy's first name. He wouldn't have gone in far. Certainly not as far as the earthworks. Or the pit. The torch flickered again. Luke shook it. The beam came on stronger, lighting a patch of the floor. Someone looked to have drawn an elongated triangle in the sand. An accident? Or Lavabo . . .? As if in answer he was sure he heard a high whimper up ahead. It was Lavabo. He recognised the tone. 'Lavabo, stay where you are.' Luke moved faster through the subterranean rooms, ranging the torch beam ahead of him. The quicker he went the quicker they would both be out of there. There was the strange junction ahead. The whimpers were getting louder. He tried to imagine Lavabo making the journey in the dark – proving his courage to him-self, attempting to earn back some self-respect. 'Are you all right? Come on. Come to me.'

It would have to be at that moment that the torch failed. The blackness was thicker than before. Somehow tangible. Luke imagined it damaging him as he inhaled, like smoke. He shook the torch. The battery rattled uselessly. The thing was not to panic. They would just turn carefully, ninety degrees, and walk. 'Lavabo, come to me.' The whimper louder now. Luke held out his hand. The fat boy grabbed it, holding firm. As he did so Luke heard Bolling calling out from above. Good. He could come and get them with his lighter.

'Guess what,' Bolling shouted, his voice small but clear, from the top of the distant stairs. 'I didn't have to search long.' Luke pulled at Lavabo, trying to move him towards the sound of another human being. 'He came back of his own accord. With half a bloody holly-bush. Didn't you,' said

Bolling, clearly addressing his words to a third party. 'What a brave old Loverboy.' It wasn't the cold hand tightening around Luke's own that so shocked him in that moment. It was the other one that came swinging around his head, fastening over his mouth, pulling him with more force than he could oppose, deeper into the impossible freezing darkness towards the waiting pit.

Come April

Tyna is a most friendly and pretty lady. Her demeanour was most accommodating. We got on so well, chatting between our 2 sessions. She kisses with enthusiasm but her absolute God's gift to men is the BBBJ performed to completion and everything swallowed with relish. It was so good that I had to have 2 helpings – well, it is Christmas after all!

Tyna (pronounced Tina) was fantastic. Really intelligent and pretty girl with lots of natural sex appeal. Forgot I was with a WG it was that good. The highlight of the evening was the BBBJ. Absolutely blinding! Deep throated me for 30 mins plus and kept the pressure perfect so I didn't come. When I did she swallowed right up to my balls and took everything. She then proceeded to milk me until I was totally spent and begged her to stop sucking. Did this twice. Would have loved to come on her face the second time but was too shy to ask. Fantastic!!!!

I met Tyna last Friday evening and what a lady, she is very friendly and extremely pleasant, I forgot that she was a working girl within minutes, which made me relax, she does most services, but I decided to try her now famous blow job, she does deepthroat and to completion, and yes I can confirm that she also swallow, she takes her time, and she really enjoy her work, unlike some other girls I met before. I will see her again and hopefully very soon, I think she was born to give blow job.

*

As Leeds' brothels went the World Famous wasn't the worst. It wasn't the best either – common consent had that down as the Calypso Studio in Gildersome. Of course the World Famous wasn't supposed to be a brothel. It advertised itself in the back of the *Yorkshire Evening Post* as an 'Executive Health Spa with full leisure facilities', but the hundreds of punters who passed through its red and black doors weren't queuing for the lone exercise bike or the feeble jacuzzi. The World Famous had a higher turnover than many of the other massage parlours and saunas in the area – and the possibility of seeing a new face was enough to keep most of its customers returning. Caprice, who now ran the place, took it over back in 1994 from an ex-nightclub bouncer called Cliff Devon. She knew what her customers liked and was good enough to her regular girls to keep them, if they wanted to stay. Some of the girls, like Tyna, had been there nearly the same length of time as Caprice (although outside the Formica-topped environs of the World Famous it's doubtful anyone would have described Tyna as a girl). Tyna herself had forgotten exactly how long she'd been working. She remembered her first week because a song called 'Country House' had been number one. The only way she'd been able to get to sleep at the time was by singing it to herself, like a prayer, and imagining the big house in the country she'd buy with all the money she was going to earn at the World Famous.

A few years later Tyna wasn't living in a big house in the country. She was living in a rented flat in Oakwood, opposite the big Tesco's. But she liked the view out of the bedroom window on to Meanwood Valley woods, particularly in the autumn when the leaves glowed orange in the morning sun. Sometimes she would stand in front of the glass, the heat from the radiator warming her chin, and imagine that Crystal was back from her foster home and that everything was going to be all right for ever. Then, like something mechanical, Tyna would turn away, pull on her long brown coat and get ready for another day's work, leaving as much of herself there as she could staring at the fiery trees.

'Can you see them now?'

Tyna was being given a piggy-back by Saffron, the chubby Indian girl from Blackburn who had only been there a week but was already a favourite with the punters. 'Over there, right at the back by the fish-tank.' They were in the girl's restroom, which backed on to the main reception. There was a window high in one wall, through which you could view the waiting area. Caprice didn't approve of this but it didn't stop the girls climbing on chairs, or each other, as in this case, in order to see who was there. It was a practice that had literally saved lives in the past, when unwanted psycho boyfriends had turned up pretending to be Johns.

'What do *they* want with me?' said Tyna.

Tyna was top of the World Famous's unofficial league table. She had more regulars than the other girls combined and since the World Famous had started its own internet site the number of those regulars had increased. The reason for Tyna's continuing popularity was the skill with which she could give a blow job. 'Oral to completion' or 'BBBJ' were the words at the bottom of her photograph, which was carefully pixellated around the eyes to disguise her identity. Tyna had only looked at the website twice but this secrecy struck her as being quite unnecessary. Who didn't know what she did for a living? Even Crystal did, which was why she'd been taken away. As for her oral skills, Tyna couldn't claim to have won them or developed them through any particular effort or practice on her part. It was just something she did. For some reason, however, the endless parade of men – fat, thin, young, old – responded in a remarkable way to the instinctive movements of her tongue and lips. Both times she had looked at the website Tyna had been amazed at the number of comments left by her satisfied customers. She tried reading them but gave up after a short while. They seemed to be talking about somebody else and it bothered her. She didn't look at the website again.

Of course it wasn't the fact that the men in the waiting room were Chinese-looking that had made Saffron so excited. They had plenty of Chinese customers. One of Tyna's regulars was an old Chinaman with a droopy moustache who Caprice called 'Fu Manchu'. No, it was rather the long coloured robes stretching from their necks to the floor. That and their clean-shaven heads.

'Ah so,' said Saffron in a cod-Oriental voice. Tyna saw that the older of the two men was barefoot. His feet stuck out from beneath the orange cloth and every so often he lifted one of them and twisted it around.

'Do you think they're in the right place? Maybe they think we're a doctor's or something,' said Tyna.

'I don't think so, dear. Unless they've both been prescribed a good sucking.' Saffron turned sharply at the voice behind her, nearly toppling Tyna on to the floor. Caprice stood in the doorway, clutching a mug of tea. 'Do you want me to send them away? They're asking if they can see you together.'

'Together!' said Saffron, giggling.

'They are offering to pay over the odds. The little one's shown me the cash.'

Tyna thought for a moment. They didn't exactly look like trouble.

'Go on, then. Give us a minute then send them up,' she said.

Tyna stopped by the kitchenette on the way up to the Hollywood Suite – the room she usually took as her own. She swilled her Tom and Jerry mug with hot water from the wall-mounted boiler and dropped in a tea bag, watching the dampness darkening the grey paper. One man, two men, Chinamen, Red Indians. At the end of the day it didn't make much difference.

She slipped on her white nurse's coat. There was a range of costumes available tucked into the cupboard under the stairs. Today she just fancied something that looked clean. She went into the Hollywood Suite and pressed the doorbell buzzer fixed near the light-switch to let Caprice know she was ready. After a few moments there was a polite knock and the two men entered. The Chinese men's robes made a swishing noise as they passed over the carpet tiles. The smaller, younger one shut the door carefully then they both turned towards Tyna and bowed.

'You are Teena?' said the younger one.

'Pleased to meet you,' she said. It was silly but she felt like she should be polite.

'I am Choma Lhari, this is my master Kyosaku Roshi.' There was a moment's silence while they looked at each other. Tyna felt she had to break it.

'And what can I do for you gents?' A gentle humming noise had begun. The older man – who now she was closer to him seemed very old indeed – had closed his eyes. He was rocking slightly, rolling gently back and forth on his heels.

'You give blow job?' said the younger man. Unusually, Tyna felt shocked. Very little shocked her, particularly where men were concerned, but it felt odd to hear those coarse words slip out of the mouth of such a religious-looking person. He, however, seemed unaware of this. His expression remained very matter of fact. The old man muttered something to him and he nodded. He removed a piece of folded paper from a pouch on his leather belt. He unfolded it. Tyna could see from the thumbprints that it had been folded and unfolded many times. The man began to read from it, struggling with some of the words: '"Wow! With day off work and nothing to do I discovered World Famous website and girl called Tyna. I was a little nervous but she put me at ease quickly. She dresses sexy but classy. What a blow job! Let me tell you this girl is going to be big! In my life very few can match this girl. Words cannot describe just how good she is at sucking cock. When I finally came it was like an out of body experience."' He looked up at her. 'This girl is you?'

There were some girls who worked at the World Famous who would be glad to accept such praise. Tyna didn't really care one way or the other, or at least normally she didn't. Standing in the presence of these unusual men, she suddenly found a name for the feeling she normally labelled as 'nothing'. It was shame. And then she realised she was doing something that she hadn't done for a long time. She was blushing. The old man opened his eyes. He looked directly at her, then pointed at the paper and pointed at her. Tyna felt she had no choice but to tell the truth. She nodded.

'My master would like you to do this for him,' said the younger man, waving the paper.

'Why?' she thought. But why was she even asking herself why? They were men. That was why. What did it matter if they were monks. Monks were still men and men liked having their cocks sucked. The old man muttered something in his cracked, throaty voice.

'My master asks if he can sit down. He is very tired.' Tyna looked at him, the deep lines round his eyes.

'Does he want to go on to the bed?' She moved some of the black satin cushions. The old man bowed his head slightly and cast himself with unexpected grace on to the sheets. He seemed to bounce as he landed, as if he weighed very little.

'We have travelled far to get here,' said the younger man. 'Once there would have been no need.' He moved to the side of the room, steadying himself against the wall. He seemed very tired too. 'There is a ceremony known as *Shakuhachi*. It can only be administered by a practised woman.' He paused, then continued. 'There are no more practised women.' The old man had closed his eyes and began his humming again. 'The ceremony of *Shakuhachi* takes man to highest plane of mind. It uses man's body against his self – in order to release the mind. What this describe', the young monk waved the paper, 'is *Shakuhachi*.'

The old man's humming had become noticeably loud. Tyna wondered if people could hear it outside. Even if they could it would hardly have stood out from the assorted grunts and groans coming from the surrounding rooms. 'We searched long to find woman who might be able to do this. Some – a very few – can do so without training. We think – from this testimony – that you are one such woman.'

'Is this a piss-take?' Tyna had only been half listening. She was trying to work out how likely this situation was. Weren't monks supposed to have given up sex? Maybe Chinky monks were different.

'*Hara, Hara*,' said the old man, who was suddenly more energetic. He had shifted up the bed, propping himself upright on his bony elbows. He was moving his robe around, trying to uncover himself. The young man looked concerned.

'You may end my master's suffering. You can help him pass over to the highest possible plane. He will have no need to come back. You will help release his soul from *Samsara*. Come.'

And now the strangest thing. Tyna felt – for the first time in a long, long while – unable to do what she was being asked. It was ridiculous. When she thought of some of the men she'd handled: the white, flabby old ones who felt like bin bags full of rotten rubbish; the ones who smelled of sweat and shit and booze and said that they loved her; the man with the beard who she had to lift out of his wheel-chair – he always wore the same underpants. All these men she had willingly taken in her mouth, happily accepting their cum in exchange for crumpled tenners. And now, faced with this holy, kind-looking old one, she felt that she couldn't. Because something about him made her aware of herself. And she was unable to bear what she felt.

The old monk had stopped humming. He was gazing at

her, suddenly seeming much younger. He shook his head and beckoned to her. He looked like a good friend.

'Come,' he said. 'Come.' She approached him. He held her hands in his. They were cold, but the way they covered hers was comforting. He spoke in his own language then looked at his younger companion.

The other monk moved towards them and said quietly, 'My master said it is not for you to decide who is of no value.' The old man looked at her smiling. It reminded Tyna of sitting on her grandmother's lap, when she was very small, feeling the woman's big bust against her head.

After a few moments at the old man's side Tyna found her hands moving into his robes. She noticed that the cloth was very fine. Within seconds she was doing what she was known for. And it didn't feel any different from how it normally felt. Except for the fact that her client stayed remarkably still – although he cried out when he came. It seemed, thought Tyna as she swallowed it down, that a Chinky monk's spunk tasted the same as everybody else's. She lifted herself up from the satin sheets. The old man lay on the bed quite still. His eyes were closed. He was smiling softly.

'My master has gone. Thank you.' Tyna looked down at the figure on the bed, who now seemed tiny among the orange robes, which spread out around him. He wasn't breathing. She pressed her hand to his cheek. It was cool. He did not move. There was no doubt that he was dead. The younger man leaned over the bed and picked up the corpse, slinging it over his shoulder. It appeared to weigh no more than a rolled-up sleeping bag. 'As he died my master said something.' The monk was at the door by now. 'He said, "God lives in your mouth".'

Tyna sat there for some time not thinking anything in particular. It felt like she'd had a dream. It was a dream she was going to keep to herself. She didn't want it to become just another story about a John, even if that was all it was. When she got home she sat by the back window with the curtains open, although it was dark. She put her hands on the radiator, allowing the warmth to spread into her. She stayed there until it started to get light and she could see the leaves in the deep blue of the dawn. She watched one fall with a surprising lack of grace. Come April the leaves would be green again and who knew where she might be.

The Coué

Charlie Thoroughgood had heard of the Coué. He knew all about its terrible provenance. But he never imagined he would gaze into its night-black eyes or be able to touch its desiccated skin with his trembling fingers.

Charlie ran his business out of a small shop on a sprawling concrete housing estate to the north of Sheffield. Saffron Lane as it was known – though there was no lane, and nothing as delicate as saffron in evidence – was one of a number of council estates built in the post-war period that was now due for demolition. Many of the residents had fled, rehoused in brighter, more anonymous accommodation. None mourned their move but Charlie himself felt a strange affection for the place. It was true he didn't have to live there – he could drive straight into a garage at the rear of his premises and avoid the rest of the estate completely, if he so wished – but there was something about the cheerless slabs and weed-cracked paving that spoke to him, and the more deserted Saffron Lane became the more he took to wandering the walkways and paths come lunchtime. He didn't care to be there after dark, but that was just expediency. Besides Janet wouldn't let him.

He'd never relied much on passing trade – obviously, since this location could hardly be expected to generate it. There were few other retailers in the vicinity, apart from an off-licence and a charity shop. But even in the days before the internet his business – 'Ubu Suku' – had built up a healthy mail-order client base. The legend beneath the logo read 'World Curios'. Charlie thought it made his enterprise sound trite but it worked as a description so he had resisted the temptation to alter it for the website.

And there was nothing trite about Charlie's expertise. His customers knew that. His depth of knowledge, his breadth of stock – his contacts and trading partners were without parallel among his peers.

The shop itself was effectively a warehouse and an office, but he liked the pretence that it was a premises for customers. He took great delight in arranging the displays, the theatre of it, making it seem as if the place was from another time – some magical Victorian emporium on Great Russell Street or in Mayfair. That was an era when collecting and classifying were seen as noble pursuits, branches of academia. A time when much of the world was still veiled in mystery and men such as Charlie were considered entrepreneurs, purveyors of enlightenment and knowledge. Though current regulations and fashionable opinion threatened to make Charlie a pariah, he persisted in his trade with a passion and bullishness his Victorian forbears would have been proud of.

When he raised the electric security shutters this particular morning, Charlie was surprised to see a figure through the painted glass of the front door. He slid the bolts carefully, then pulled the door towards him. The man, for it was a man, almost fell inside. He had been facing the other way, studying the desolate concrete concourse. He turned and grinned foolishly, revealing a set of prominent teeth. They were arranged in an unusually sharp curve, suggesting a physiognomy more rodent than human. He looked academic, and gentrified, so it was a surprise to hear a heavy Essex accent when he spoke.

'Mr Thoroughgood?'

'Yes,' said Charlie.

'Mr Charles Thoroughgood?' The 'Charles' emphasised as if there might be a hundred Thoroughgoods in the vicinity but only one of any fame and distinction.

'Yes,' said Charlie again, determined to offer no more. The man held out his hand. It was narrow and girlish, but the skin was rough and calloused, the fingertips stained and sore-looking. Charlie gave it a perfunctory shake.

'Collins. Rudolph Collins. It's an honour, sir. A pleasure and an honour.' The man bustled inside. He carried several bags – mostly of the battered-looking polythene variety, though there was one large canvas item, like an old-fashioned camper's. 'It took a little initiative to get here,' he said, laying the bags down. 'A map of the local bus services got me so far, but I'm afraid I made several wrong turns.' He looked up at Charlie. 'Still,' he said, suddenly smiling, 'I'm here now.' Charlie tried to busy himself around the shop, moving behind the main counter, withdrawing a pile of invoices from beneath a paperweight. But Mr Collins moved towards him, reaching for the paperweight, cupping it in his hand. It was a block of crystal containing a large black spider. '*Haplopelma minax*,' he said. 'Female. Very nasty.' Again the big grin revealing the inhuman teeth.

'And how can I help Mr . . .?' said Charlie, trying not to sound in any way friendly. He was suspicious of the man and hoped that he would leave. He would be quite happy to turn away the custom.

'Collins. Rudolph Collins,' said the man again. He put the paperweight down and stepped forward, his own face stopping just short of Charlie's. His breath smelled of peppermints, and something worse beneath. 'If I was to say the word "Coué" to you,' said the man, 'what would you think?'

'I'm sorry,' Charlie said.

'Come come, Mr Thoroughgood. You've heard of the Coué, I'm sure of that.' He smiled again. Charlie thought about the man's skull, what it would look like stripped of skin and cartilage. Not quite human.

'I couldn't get you one. It's against the law to trade such an item.' No need to play games with the man. Charlie smelled entrapment. Let's speed through this charade, he thought, and get him off the premises.

'So you do know what I'm talking about.' The man raised his eyebrows. He didn't conceal his excitement.

'There's nothing more to discuss,' said Charlie. He turned away from the man, standing upright. He picked up the pile of invoices again. Mr Collins stayed where he was, studying Charlie as he moved away from behind the desk.

'Oh, I know you couldn't get me one. I wouldn't expect to come here and have you get me one. One doesn't wander into a shop – even a shop such as this – and say, excuse me, I would like a Coué please. In fact I'll take two, if you have them.'

'To tell you the truth, Mr . . . Collins, I doubt that such a thing actually exists.'

'Indeed. Yes. I doubted that the Hand of Glory actually existed. Until I located one in the private collection of a Mr Ammar from Whitby. It sits now, as we speak, on the mantel-piece in my study. I don't ever light it of course. I might fall asleep and never wake up.' Charlie wasn't going to respond to such a lure. He moved towards the office area, beneath the shelf of puffer fish. 'But the Coué . . .' the man had no inten-tion of shutting up. 'The Coué does exist. You see I have one with me. Here. In this bag. I was wondering if you might like to buy it.' He smiled like a conjurer pulling something delightful from an empty box.

'What?'

'Come come, Mr Thoroughgood. I'm offering you a once in a lifetime opportunity.' There was something fervent about his entreaty. Something desperate.

'I'm a businessman. What good is there in stock I can't sell on?'

The Coué

'Mr Thoroughgood—'

'Thank you. I've a very busy morning ahead.'

'Mr—'

'Thank you.'

Later, after the man had left, Charlie went into his office and sat looking at the photo of Janet above the computer. She was thinner then – good looking. Less flesh on her face. He could just imagine what she might have to say were he to spend a thousand pounds on such an item. Not that he would have done so. He had refused even to look at it.

'This came for you.' It was the first thing she said to him when he got home. Janet was holding an envelope. It was grubby and brown, like it had been forgotten at the bottom of a bag for a year or so.

'What do you mean "came for me"?'

'You're in a good mood. Charming.' She walked over and pressed her lips wetly against his cheek, giving him a half-comical kiss. He took the envelope, watching her go across the room. Her big arse. The idea of touching it momentarily repulsed him. 'I've been speaking to your mother,' she said.

'What?'

'About child care.' Charlie didn't respond. He examined the envelope – the slanting handwriting. 'She thinks she could manage two days.'

'And the other three?' he said. 'It's thousands. In a year. If we pay for it. It adds up, you know.'

'Charlie. We'll find a way. Everybody manages.' Charlie looked inside the envelope. A lone business card, tatty and dog-eared. Rudolph Collins. A mobile number written on the back. 'Call me.'

Later, sitting in his room. His private room, surrounded by his personal collection. It was where he felt safest, among his things. The ivory puzzle balls. The lizard skeletons. The two-headed calf that had been on display at Ripley's Believe it or Not in Hollywood. He reached for a book from the shelf above the display cabinets. Lewis Spence's *Encyclopaedia of Occultism*. It was a long time since he'd opened it. It had been a favourite of his childhood. He remembered a long summer's day. Nine years old. Cricket at school in the afternoon. It seemed strange now, his childhood interest in something so esoteric. It had felt so normal at the time. He leafed through the pages. There was a woodcut of the Hand of Glory. Like the one that supposedly resided on Rudolph Collins's mantelpiece. He had wanted nothing more than to see such a thing as a child. The idea of owning one would have been quite unbelievable. He flicked further on. A blade of long grass caught in the junction of paper and binding. The entry for the Coué. An engraving of the hideous curled-up thing. 'The Coué is the mummified body of a baby – a girl-child of less than six months bred and then slaughtered . . .' A rhythmic knock.

'Chuck?' The door opened. Janet's face, plump and round, filling the crack. She edged her way within tentatively. 'Do you want an Options?' She held out a steaming mug – a sickly butterscotch smell rising from it. Charlie shut the book. 'Maybe I could work part-time. If I go freelance. I could earn more money in three days than I do in five.'

Charlie tapped the computer keyboard making the screen spring into life, hoping that she wouldn't notice it had been in sleep mode. He nodded.

'Maybe. Let's think about it. Do some sums.'

'Charlie.' He sipped at the hot chocolate, tasted powder. He could hear the waver in her voice. Knew that if she sensed his ambivalence she would be upset. He reached out for her and squeezed her arm.

'No, really,' he said. 'We will.'

She looked around at the collection. 'It's time you got rid of all this. You know that, don't you.' She pulled her arm away from his and walked out.

'Mr Collins?' Charlie hadn't expected him to answer. 'Are you still here?'

'Mr Thoroughgood. I can be with you this afternoon. This afternoon.'

And Rudolph Collins was there that afternoon in the same clothes as before, still carrying his polythene bags. Charlie wouldn't have been surprised to find he'd been sleeping under a bridge.

'I took the liberty of bringing my own cup of tea. I hope you don't mind.' He held out a polystyrene cup. He pulled at the cover. His hands were shaking. He looked sweaty and ill. He sipped at the drink, drawing it through his ratty teeth.

'And have you got the . . . Are you still willing to sell—'

'Oh yes, Mr Thoroughgood,' said Collins, looking over his shoulder. 'I'm willing to sell. I'm ready and willing to sell.' He hauled his canvas bag up on to the desk. Putting down his tea he began to work at the buckles, fingers moving quickly and eagerly, despite the tremens. He withdraw a large object packed in newspaper. He quickly tore the stuff away like a child playing pass the parcel. Underneath was an elegant cherry-wood box. He pushed it slightly towards Charlie. 'I'm only asking a thousand, you understand. I'm barely making a profit.' Charlie nodded. Mr Collins unwrapped a mint and pushed it in his mouth. He took another gulp of tea. 'But I need the money, you see. An unexpectedly high tax bill. Death and taxes, Mr Thoroughgood.' Charlie's hand drifted over the box's burnished brass catches.

'A thousand?'

'Yes, I really can't afford to go any lower.'

Charlie flicked the catch and raised the lid. Inside was a large glass bell jar, surrounded by black silk, nestling in a hollowed out inversion of its own shape.

'Eight hundred, then,' said Mr Collins. Charlie hadn't challenged his original price. The expanse of preserved skin visible through the glass was yellow in colour, buttery but dry like pastry. The thing's back. Charlie shut the lid. He looked at Mr Collins.

'Seven hundred and fifty. I will not go any lower.'

'The box is very beautiful.'

'Oh yes. Specially made. By its second owner. Shall we say seven-fifty?' Collins's breathing was shallow and excited.

'And where did you come by it?'

'An auction.'

'An auction!'

'Very recently. In Morocco. A private affair. For collectors.' Charlie touched the case. The wood was warm. Smooth as the silk lining inside.

'Seven-fifty?'

'Cash,' said Collins, adding quickly, 'if that's OK with you.' Charlie looked up at him, his grey-stubbled, flatiron-shaped face. The stained brim of his hat. No wife to care for him. Perhaps no friend in the world.

'I'm devoted to my collection. It pains me to part with anything. But items such as this can command too high a price.' Charlie nodded as he pulled open the drawer, withdrawing the cash box. 'A receipt. If you could make out a receipt. As proof of the sale.' Collins made a great fuss of the particulars. The spelling of his name and address, and the fullness of Charlie's own details. 'And if you could just sign there. Your signature at the bottom.' As Charlie handed him the paper, Collins seemed to lighten, his bones and muscles loosening, releasing knotted elements of himself. 'A fine transaction, Mr Thoroughgood, a fine transaction. I'm sure it won't be long before you've sold the item on – at profit. Considerable profit.'

'I'm not selling it on,' said Charlie. Collins looked at him, surprised. 'This is for me.'

'What you got there?'

'Work,' said Charlie, clutching the bulky bag to his chest.

'Let's have a look.'

'Do you want a take-away?'

'Chuck. I'm trying to lose weight.' Charlie struggled up the stairs. The semi was small. Had become too small even for the two of them. Ten years of living there together and they had accumulated too much stuff. He made it on to the landing without her seeing what was in the large carrier bag. He'd wrapped the box inside a blanket. He couldn't have left it in the shop, the risk of a Trading Standards inspection discovering it was too great. Besides it belonged to him. He wanted it at home.

'I'll be down in a minute.' There was access to the loft via his room. A painted plywood panel that lifted up. He could keep it up there in its bag, wrapped in the blanket. She would never have to know. She was too fat to fit through the trapdoor. It was a risk bringing it home like this but he wanted to look at it, examine it properly, relax in its presence. Something had kept him from doing so in the shop. He sat on the floor with his back against the door. If Janet tried to come in he would have enough time to push it under the blanket. He gathered some other, more innocuous items around himself. He unclipped the fastenings of the box. Who would have fashioned the item with such care? The bell jar reflected the light fitting above it. Charlie shifted on his haunches. He reached into the box, feeling the smoothness of the silk against the back of his hands. Carefully, ensuring his grip was firm, he extracted the glass case from its holding. There was a little rush of air as he did so, a crackle of static electricity. The Coué's back was still facing him. He placed it down on the carpet. Slowly, with two hands, he rotated the jar towards himself. The first thing he registered were its tiny hands, almost vestigial, like a dinosaur's. He didn't want to look into its face. He'd expected the eyes to be closed, but they were open. Staring up at him. The sockets beneath were black. Impulsively he tapped on the glass. It sounded distinctively. Tink tink tink. The legs vibrated, curled into the dry, crispy belly. Each individual toe was discernible. The hair on its head was wispy and feathery, like a very old man's. He looked at it for a few moments longer then lifted the bell jar back into its box.

*

'Darling?'

'Hmmm.'

'Are you asleep?'

'Hmmm.'

'Chuck.' She knew he was cross about something. Knew he was sulking. He had waited downstairs, sat with his legs over the arm of the chair, flicking through the channels on the Freeview, listening to her preparations for bed. The clink of crockery going into the dishwasher, the boiling of the kettle, the water running into the bathroom sink. He'd let her climb the stairs, grunting that he'd be up in a minute. The Coué had already been placed in the loft, the beautiful cherry-wood box wrapped in a blanket. Eventually he ascended himself, sat on the lavatory seat, running the electric toothbrush over his teeth. Now he lay in bed, pretending to have fallen immediately into a deep sleep. He thought about the night they first slept together. He hadn't wanted her then. She had chased him on to the bus. He'd tried to tell her he didn't want to go out with her, didn't want to see her. But she'd chased him anyway and told him that she was going home with him. And he'd assented. 'Let's have a look at you,' she'd said as they lay naked, and he'd felt violated somehow, horribly exposed. He'd sworn to never let it happen again. But then it had. And one day he'd found himself feeling fonder about her. He'd veer between one and the other – the repulsion and the attraction. Part of him had craved it when she suggested moving in together. But somewhere, something inside him had vowed that he would not marry her. He didn't love her. He had to believe he could walk away. He wanted to know he could walk back to that past. Lying on the lawn. Just him. And dream of his things. The things he loved. The life he loved.

'Darling?' She sounded sleepy now. This time he didn't even grunt. She desisted from questioning him. Outside a lone car drove past, tyres rolling across the tarmac.

Later he woke. He couldn't see the time. The bulk of her

body between him and the digital clock. It lit the room with a soft greenish tinge. The little house silent around him. And then, somewhere above, a distant, percussive beat. It stopped. Was that what woke him? How could it? It seemed so quiet, so delicate. He lay absolutely still, trying to listen to the house around him over Janet's heavy respiration. It came again. Precise, familiar. Tink tink tink. He stiffened, sat upright. Held his breath, desperate to hear. The noise did not resume, unless that was it, starting up once more as sleep took him. A beetle trapped in a cup. Tink. Tink. Tink.

Charlie was surprised when he arrived at the shop the next morning to find a visitor waiting for him once again. This time, however, the figure was uniformed. A lone policeman. Charlie's first thought was that there'd been a break-in, or some trouble on the estate. His second, rather melodramatically was about the Coué, and he was grateful that he had taken it home, that it was safely hidden wrapped in the innocuous white blanket. But, it transpired, the visit was on account of another matter entirely.

'Do you recognise him?' The question repeated, a little too insistently, the policeman studying Charlie as he in turn studied the photo on the counter. It was Collins. Again Charlie thought about the Coué. Its tiny hands clasped to its desiccated chest.

'No,' he said, attempting to look the policeman straight in the eye. The man looked young to him. Bored. On a routine assignment.

'Are you sure, sir?'

Charlie's Blackberry buzzed inside his jacket. He pulled it out, laid it on the counter without looking at it. 'Pretty sure. What's he done?'

'Died, sir.' This said dryly and without irony. Charlie peered at the photo again. He didn't want to speak but he tried to contort his face into an expression that said, maybe I did know him; let me have a better look.

'He was found with your address in his wallet. There seemed no other reason for his presence in the area.'

'Ummm . . .'

'There is an independent witness who claims to have seen him hanging around the entrance to your shop yesterday morning.'

'How did he die?'

'We found him at Victoria Quays.'

'Drowned?'

'No. He was at the water's edge but he hadn't jumped in. We don't know the cause of death.' The policeman studied Charlie. 'Yet.'

'It's him.' Charlie winced at the weakness of his own volte-face.

'So you do recognise him, sir?'

'There was a man here yesterday. I thought he was mad. Or drunk. I sent him away.'

'What did he want?'

'He was selling. Or so he said. I wasn't interested.'

'So there was no transaction between you?'

'Oh no. It was all clearly dodgy. Furs. Ivory. Wouldn't touch it with a barge-pole.' Charlie thought about the canal. Collins dropping dead.

'You bought nothing from him.'

'No. You're quite free to look around.'

'We found a large amount of cash on him.'

Charlie shrugged his shoulders. 'As I say. You're quite free to look around.' The policeman turned his head, looked around the shop at the hardwood display cases and pictures.

'I assume you have an alibi for your whereabouts last night.'

'What?'

The policeman turned back to look at Charlie. He couldn't have been more than thirty.

'Yes.' Charlie tried not to bristle too much. 'I was with my partner . . . my girlfriend. At home.' The policeman nodded.

'I just need to take some contact details then, sir. If we want to speak to you again.'

Charlie left work early that day. He'd half-heartedly completed a number of orders, one of which needed parcel-posting to the US. The trip to the post office was an excuse to bunk off. Why was Collins dead? It was true he'd looked ill when Charlie had arrived. He wished he hadn't bought the thing off him now. Couldn't understand what pleasure he had thought owning it would bring. He sat in the car for a moment before starting it up. His heart was palpitating. There was a sense of being in trouble. As if he'd done something terribly wrong. But he hadn't. Collins was selling the thing. Charlie had bought it. He hadn't killed anyone. He would get rid of it. Throw it in the canal. And that would be the end of the matter. The garage beyond the windscreen suddenly seemed very dark. Something scratched at a shadowed wall. He turned on his headlamps, illuminating cobwebbed shelves.

Janet wasn't in when he got home. He took himself up to his room, not seeing the boxes with his exhibits in them, only the shadows between them. He turned on the two table-lamps and the angle-poise fastened to the bookshelf. Then he took a chair and stood on it, carefully lifting the square of painted plywood in the ceiling. Standing on his tip-toes he peered into the loft space. There was the box, still wrapped in its blanket, just where it had been the night before. He reached for it lifting it down into the room. He threw it on to the spare bed. It bounced for a moment before settling, making a depression in the centre of the duvet. Quickly, not wanting to, he uncoiled the blanket and lifted the catches on the box. The bell jar rested within, exactly as it had done when he had last looked at it. He turned it around, staring into the scrunched-up face of the little thing inside. When he was a kid he had made himself shrunken heads for Halloween. Apples covered in clear nail varnish with little faces carved in them. He had dried them in the airing cupboard. His simulations had been accurate it seemed. The face scowled up at him. Was it furious? Or in pain? It had not moved since he had last looked. Did he think that it would have done?

Janet had made dinner. Laid the table. He was thankful that she hadn't lit a candle.

'I'm sorry, Chuck. I know you think I'm obsessed.'

'No.' It was a fish pie. She'd drawn lines in the mash potato with a fork before grilling it. He began bisecting the lines across the grain with his own fork. Making little dashed slices. 'A man died today.'

'What? Who?'

'Last night. One of my suppliers.'

'Chuck. I'm sorry.'

'I didn't like him. Barely knew him.'

'Still. How old was he?'

'He wasn't married.'

'Are you all right?' There was a pause. Charlie looked down at the tiny pieces of pie that he'd carved. He pushed a few of them across the plate, his fork scraping the china.

'I don't want to have a baby, Janet,' he said, clearly, firmly. The central heating boiler clicked into life in the kitchen. He heard the roar of the gas. Imagined the flame burning blue. 'I don't love you,' he said, without looking at her.

He checked into the Pennine Way Hotel. He'd stayed there before, when the water mains had burst. They both had. It would only be for a night or two. He lay back on the bed. The room smelled of air freshener and ancient cigarettes. He'd tried going to sleep with the television on, but sleep wouldn't come. Reluctantly, he turned the lights off. It wasn't dark. There was an illuminated strip beneath the doorway. Light came through the thin orange curtains. He must have dropped off for he awoke suddenly, feeling panicky and disorientated.

The Coué

He didn't know where he was. He thought he saw something sitting on a chair in the corner of the room. Something little. Looking at him. He fumbled for the switch. Of course there was nothing apart from his balled-up overcoat. The hotel seemed very quiet. A distant roar from the M1. Another noise started up, light and percussive. A repetitive tinkle. It seemed familiar, a beat he'd heard before. He closed his eyes and tried to ignore it. Except when he did that it sounded as if it were outside his window. He was on the third floor. Nothing could get in. But then he remembered the front of the hotel. The extended block protruding into the car park. He was reluctant to open the curtains. The rhythm became more insistent. Eventually he got out of bed and threw the thin fabric aside. A heavy union flag shook in the wind, mounted on a portion of flat roof, just beyond the glass. Steel cable rattled against the metal eyelet sewn into its corner.

Charlie went back to collect the Coué from the house the next morning. The circumstances of his leaving had been hurried – there hadn't been time to get into the loft. Janet left for work at seven-fifteen. Checking her car wasn't outside, Charlie slipped within.

The hallway was dark, almost like night. It was a gloomy morning, the clouds dirty and low outside. His first thought was that Janet was still there. It felt like someone was upstairs. He stood still, halting his breathing, straining to hear any sign of occupancy, readying himself to run. He did not want to replay a line of their last conversation.

Nothing. The house was as silent as falling snow.

Carefully he climbed the staircase. As he did so he was gripped with an intense feeling that he shouldn't be there, as if something violent were waiting for him in the bedroom. Fully alert he rose on to the cheerless landing. There was a dark figure leaning against the bath – arms outstretched, yearning, reaching for him. He only had to move a fraction to correct his misperception. It was the shower curtain, bunched awkwardly, its wetness gluing it in an odd position to the side of the tub. Janet must have left in a hurry that morning. She was normally so conscientious about keeping each room tidy. Moving as quickly as he could Charlie retrieved the shrouded box from the attic. He would wait for a brighter day before collecting the rest of his things.

He'd take the Coué to the canal later in the morning. Maybe not the canal. Maybe the river. He'd grab a vinyl sack from the back of the shop, weigh it down with bricks. He looked over his shoulder as he slammed the car door shut. He was glad he could pull right into his garage. He hadn't felt safe since he'd walked out of the hotel. Maybe the police had been watching him. It was ridiculous. How could he be a suspect? A bottle toppled over somewhere in the darkness. He should clear the place out, now that the estate was emptying. He didn't want rats in the shop.

He found himself on the internet again all morning. There was an amount of work that he should be doing but he'd started a thread on one of the esoteria forums and wanted to watch its development.

Gothichost.net > Forum Index > General Mythology

Chunnelgood
Member

Joined March 2001
Posts 271

Posted Fri Feb 11, 2006, 9:08 am Post subject Coué facts

Wondered if anyone had any experience or any knowledge about the Coué or any related stories? Anyone know of anybody who owns or has owned a Coué?

The Coué

Turglover
Member

Joined Feb 2003
Posts 64

Posted Fri Feb 11, 2006, 10:11 am Post subject Coué facts

You joke with me Chunnelgood man right. There ain't no such thing as a Coué.

Life is a waste of time, time is a waste of time. Get wasted all of the time and you'll have the time of your life!

Chunnelgood
Member

Joined March 2001
Posts 272

Posted Fri Feb 11, 2006, 10:15 am Post subject Coué facts

Coué does exist. Have seen photographs. That aside wondered if anyone had any stories or knew any mythology.

Eldritch Nut-cache
Member

Joined August 2002
Posts 98

Posted Fri Feb 11, 2006, 10:18 am Post subject Coué facts

The Coué destroys. Takes from you. He who owns the
Coué carries the weight.

*'Ten million ships on fire. The entire Dalek race wiped out
in one second . . . I watched it happen. I MADE it happen!'*

Turglover
Member

Joined Feb 2003
Posts 65

Posted Fri Feb 11, 2006, 10:33 am Post subject Coué
facts

You ain't seen no photographs man. F**k that s**t!!!

*Life is a waste of time, time is a waste of time. Get
wasted all of the time and you'll have the time of your life!*

Chunnelgood
Member

Joined March 2001
Posts 273

Posted Fri Feb 11, 2006, 10:37 am Post subject Coué
facts

Eldritch. What is the weight you carry if you own the
Coué?

The Coué

Eldritch Nut-cache
Member

Joined August 2002
Posts 99

Posted Fri Feb 11, 2006, 10:39 am Post subject Coué facts

The Coué was made to take. It draws it out of you like salt draws water. It feeds on that which you love the most.

'Ten million ships on fire. The entire Dalek race wiped out in one second … I watched it happen. I MADE it happen!'

Turglover
Member

Joined Feb 2003
Posts 66

Posted Fri Feb 11, 2006, 10:58 am Post subject Coué facts

You guys crack me up.

Life is a waste of time, time is a waste of time. Get wasted all of the time and you'll have the time of your life!

Charlie wondered how quickly he could find a buyer. It wasn't something that he could go on the open market with. Anyway he would pay to get rid of the thing. He remembered how carefully Collins had made him fill out the receipt. The patient requests for exact details. It couldn't be a simple matter of just dumping it. If that had been the case Collins would have dropped it in the canal himself. He wondered how carefully Collins had selected him – how much research he'd done. Had Charlie been the perfect candidate? He felt as if he didn't have that luxury himself. He needed to be rid of the Coué and now. Every second between him and being free of it felt as if it multiplied the danger. Danger? Danger of what? He looked around the shop – the neatly arranged cases, the patchwork colours of the exhibits within. The plethora of items carefully ordered on shelves and bookcases. The room felt very dark. Charlie switched on an extra light.

You would think it would be easy to divest yourself of something. Anything. Smash it up. Burn it. Bury it. But to transfer ownership. That was another matter. He decided to go for a walk around the estate.

To the left of the concourse two shaven-headed boys kicked a tennis ball back and forth between them. Not yet teenagers they had an air of brutality about them. They didn't look up as he passed. Their ball thumped repeatedly against the brickwork. A glacial February wind blew. Charlie pulled himself into the wall. Another sound came towards him, echoing off the high concrete. A distant percussive tapping. Something hard against glass. It shared the rhythm of the boys' ball. There was the charity shop on the far side of the estate, where it met the main road. If he went to them with a pre-printed form – he could knock it up on the computer – they would only have to sign. A record of ownership having passed. He was sure he could convince them. He turned a corner into one of the walkways – a narrow flyover that ran above the service road beneath. It was long and narrow, fashioned from dirty concrete and breezeblocks. He tried to walk as fast as he could. The wind caught some litter behind him. A glass bottle rolled across the pathway, or so it sounded. It must have had a lump on it, some irregularity. It sounded each time it hit the ground. Something struck Charlie in the chest, come to life, caught in his clothes. His Blackberry. He'd set it to email him if the forum was updated. He carried on walking as he pulled it out, running the thumb-wheel down.

S
Guest

Joined Feb 2006
Posts 1

Posted Fri Feb 11, 2006, 11:57 am Post subject Coué facts

The Coué is not the thing. The Coué was made to make something else. The Coué merely calls for it.

Charlie had had enough of this now. He put the Blackberry back in his pocket. He was taking the necessary action. And then he'd be done with it.

It was all superstitious nonsense. Ridiculous, superstitious nonsense. The appeal of the collection to him was ironic, not magical. He had no interest in such thinking. He pushed open the door to the charity shop. He had been in a number of times before, just in case he might uncover an item of real value. Such accidental finds were rare, but did happen. He spent a moment at a rail of peppery-smelling clothes, flicking across the brown faded jackets and wrinkled, off-white shirts. Then he approached the old woman behind the cash register, who was occupied flattening out some metallic wrapping paper.

'Is there an Esme works here?' said Charlie, as convinc-ingly as he could manage.

'Sorry, love?'

'Does Esme work here? I had something for her.'

'I only come in of a Monday.' The woman wasn't interested in Charlie. The paper was far more interesting to her.

'I had an item for her. A box I'd promised she could sell on. Could I bring it round for her later.'

'Do what you like, love.'

'That's very kind of you. What's your name?'

The woman looked up at him again. Her skin looked as grey as her hair. She might have been fifty or seventy. It depended on her diet, how much she drank.

'Juliet,' she said. She eyed him suspiciously.

'Not Juliet Gardener.' For a minute Charlie thought she wouldn't take the bait.

'Forester.'

'Forester.'

'I don't know you,' said the old woman indignantly.

'Christopher. Christopher Trace. I'll be back with it shortly.' He smiled, in as friendly a manner as he could.

It felt like it was getting dark when he got back to the shop. He didn't want to go into the garage to get the thing. He left the door open when normally he might shut it, allowing what pale daylight there was to disperse the shadows. He hurriedly retrieved the paper bag from the boot.

He didn't want to look at it again. He didn't even want to take off the blanket. He went about creating the document first. There was no need for it to be complicated.

'I Charles Louis Thoroughgood transfer all rights of ownership of this item to Juliet Forester this 11th day of February 2006.'

He printed out the paper. The thought occurred to him, what if Juliet – or one of the other women – opened the box and on finding the document were so horrified at the awful thing that they called the police. He went and retrieved his toolbox from the back office.

He removed the bell jar, keeping the Coué turned away from him. With a scalpel he carefully worked a piece of the black silk away from the wood. Then using a small bit on the power drill he hollowed out a shallow well in the exposed mahogany. He cut the printed document into a small strip containing the text, rolling it into a pellet. Delicately he inserted the pellet into the well and filled it with epoxy resin. Then he reattached the silk, using a small dab of Magna-Tac. He left it to dry. Of course this was all ridiculous. He was merely doing it for his peace of mind.

He found another box, a cardboard box. He placed the blanket-wrapped bundle inside and taped the whole package up tightly. In block capitals, on the side, he wrote 'Esme'.

He drove round to the main road. He was worried the woman would be gone and he would find the charity shop all locked up. But it was still open, fluorescent lights flickering painfully. He insisted on carrying the box through into the back. Wouldn't hear of Juliet carrying it. He was relying on her fecklessness. As he had hoped she stayed at her till, reading her *Star* and eating Maltesers. The chaotic nature of the stock room was a gift to him. There was an old wardrobe in the corner. Checking the door as he went, Charlie hurriedly pushed a table across the room and stood on it, chucking the box on top of the wardrobe and pushing it back as far as he could against the wall. He leaped down, pulled the table back to its original position and satisfied himself that the box could not be seen. It was perfectly possible that it would stay there unnoticed for several years.

There was nothing immoral about his actions because it was all just nonsense. He had achieved peace of mind. He had divested himself of the vile item. He had spoken the truth to Janet. Everything was clean.

He thought he would stay in the shop for a while. He might search online for some temporary accommodation, somewhere to rent until he and Janet had resolved what to do with the house. He clicked on Firefox and began to type into Google. As he did the address bar brought up a list of other sites, Gothichost being the uppermost. Idly he scrolled down and clicked. Feeling freer now he was curious to see how the chat might have progressed.

Eldritch Nut-cache
Member

Joined August 2002
Posts 99

Posted Fri Feb 11, 2006, 10:39 am Post subject Coué facts

The Coué was made to take. It draws it out of you like salt draws water. It feeds on that which you love the most.

'Ten million ships on fire. The entire Dalek race wiped out in one second … I watched it happen. I MADE it happen!'

Turglover
Member

Joined Feb 2003
Posts 66

Posted Fri Feb 11, 2006, 10:58 am Post subject Coué facts

You guys crack me up.

Life is a waste of time, time is a waste of time. Get wasted all of the time and you'll have the time of your life!

The Coué

Posted Fri Feb 11, 2006, 11:57 am Post subject Coué facts

The Coué is not the thing. The Coué was made to make something else. The Coué merely calls for it.

Posted Fri Feb 11, 2006, 12:17 am Post subject Coué facts

Correct. The Mother that bred it. Who is black with hate.

'Oh no tears please, it's a waste of good suffering'

His phone went. It was Janet. He switched it off. For the first time in the day he thought about her. Felt the tension in his stomach. But he was relieved. Relieved to be alone. He would go out in a minute. The off-licence would be open. He might buy himself a bottle of wine. There was only one thing left that irritated him. Why had Collins died? He stopped the thoughts, ceasing them with his will. The curse was nonsensical. Besides, Collins had already sold the thing. Surely he should have been free. Of course he was free. He had always been free. The man just died. That was all.

Janet put down the phone. He wasn't going to answer, was he? Let that be it, then. She didn't believe him, though. She knew Charlie. Knew that he didn't know his own mind. His own heart. She went down to the kitchen and turned on the light. What she saw was black, like a bat and bigger than her. It shouldn't have been able to move the way it did. She screamed so hard that it hurt her throat. And then it was on her, so no one would have heard a thing.

Bound South

'Do I contradict myself? Very well I contradict myself.
(I am large. I contain multitudes.)
Walt Whitman

It was the winter of 1913, mid-February to be precise, and I was making my first journey to our capital city. The newspapers were full of Captain Scott's death and I was hoping to attend his memorial service at St Paul's. This, I must add, was not the reason behind the trip though I had followed Scott's fortunes since his initial attempt to reach the Pole a decade earlier. I am prepared to accept, however, that my romantic view of his exploits may well have fuelled the motor of my own mission south.

I was twenty-two – which viewed from this perspective feels like childhood, but at the time seemed grand and old and wise. I was travelling to the Admiralty and an interview with Captain Sir George Mansfield Smith-Cumming about a position in a new division known only euphemistically as the 'Service' or the 'Bureau'. The information I had about it was decidedly sketchy. My family had no history of military involvement – indeed quite the opposite since my father was a prominent Quaker. My expertise was in the area of modern European languages, which I had studied to an unusually advanced level, having taken the Kinnessburn Prize at St Andrews two years previously. It was this, combined with a recommendation from my Professor, that had led Mansfield Smith-Cumming to seek me out.

It has to be said, I didn't take much persuading. My favourite book at this time was Kipling's *Kim*. Thoughts of covert operations and concealed identities were delicious and enticing, not that Smith-Cumming's letter had even hinted at such things. It was my own reading and interpretation of his 'matters of the nation's and His Majesty's most supreme interest' that led to this perception. There were other reasons for pursuing the position – personal reasons which I will elaborate on as this narrative progresses – but at this point it is enough to know that I thought, most vigorously, that I was in the service of a Higher Power.

My train departed from Waverley Station at seventeen minutes past seven a.m. The journey was some eight and a half hours and though the Admiralty had offered to reimburse me, it was only for the amount of a third-class ticket, so I had developed a plan to secure more comfortable arrangements for at least some of the duration by taking a seat in one of the dining cars and spinning out breakfast for a couple of hours. I confess I was unfamiliar with the ins and outs of making such a long journey but this advice I had received from my good friend Munroe Porde – a man who liked to think of himself as a sophisticate, which, compared with me at least, he was.

The first mistake I made was boarding the wrong carriage. I had to dismount and make my way to the other end of the platform. Within seconds of alighting again the engine had begun its slow creep out of the city making it even harder to find where I was supposed to be going. My self-consciousness inhibited me from asking one of the guards, or indeed another passenger, where the dining car might be found. I was determined for it to appear that I had a precise agenda and thus affected to move with confidence along the narrow corridors.

Bound South

It was not possible then, as it has become in more recent times, to navigate from one end of the train to the other. In fact the vehicle was comprised of discrete clusters of interconnected carriages, mostly grouped in pairs or trios. One could pass through the vestibule that connected the individual coaches, but when the next vestibule was reached one found oneself faced with a sealed door, or indeed no door at all. To get from one group of carriages to another, there was no choice but to wait until the train was standing in a station. It was on this topological quirk that Munroe Porde's dodge was based. If you settled in the dining car the guards would not check your ticket, or if they did they would tolerate your presence so long as you returned to third at the first available point after you had eaten. Needless to say if one lingered over breakfast, perhaps a quarter of the journey could have been covered before one found oneself back in less salubrious and less comfortable surroundings.

The particular dining car I found myself in may have not been the place that Munroe Porde had in mind when he made his suggestion, which accounts for what follows, and indeed the whole curious story that I'm about to relate. The surroundings were indeed grand – mahogany walls, pigskin upholstery and a relief-printed linoleum on the floor, which gave the effect of enamelled tiling. There were electric lights throughout and a small clerestory roof with ducts that piped out warm air from some kind of central heating system. I tried to adopt a confident pose as if I belonged completely in this environment. The smell of kippers and gammon emerged from the kitchen area, and beneath that the slightly acrid scent of the oil-fired range.

Inevitably as the soot-blackened trees passed by the window, my mind drifted to thinking about my father. It was three weeks since we had spoken. Perhaps I had hoped for some rapprochement before I left. In truth my own pride prevented it. I was dimly aware of this even then. But I had the certainty of right on my side – or so I told myself. My father

139

was an old man, naive and small-minded, unable to see the greater good that was clear to me. He was ill-educated, or at least not university-educated, having made his fortune in trade. And as for the pacifism dictated by his beliefs – well, it was nonsensical. Worse, it was untenable. One had to fight, for conflict was a necessary condition of being in this imperfect world. There was a new materialism afoot that would save us from the superstition and darkness of the past to which my father was still bound in his own peculiar way. I was something new. I had a vision. A twentieth-century vision. The future lay in good government, in political science, in economics, industry too. As Von Bismarck had observed, the lubrication this new machinery of state required was *realpolitik* – and to exercise *realpolitik* effectively a government needed reliable intelligence. If I could contribute to this in any way, I had a duty to do so. Rarefied and antiquated moralities could not block that path, indeed it would have been an immorality to let them do so.

These thoughts were disturbed by an altercation at the other end of the dining car. Two guards were leaning over a lone passenger, a little older than myself. It was hard to hear their conversation for they were speaking in deliberately lowered voices. Occasionally the passenger raised his own voice but he was quickly subdued by one of the officials, who had a hand rested firmly on his shoulder. The traveller made a show of searching in his pockets, patting breast then hip with left and then right hand. It was clear that they were demanding to see his ticket and even clearer that he was dissembling in some manner. I watched these events with quickening heart. A brief glance around the rest of the passengers was enough to convince me of the grand folly of my scheme. The finery on display, the quality of apparel not to mention the demeanour of the individuals themselves, meant that this other man, and myself too, stood out like a dollop of manure on freshly swept cobbles. Whatever Munroe Porde's experience had been it must have been very different from this. As the guards lifted the straying passenger bodily to his feet, removing him from the carriage in a none-too-friendly manner I realised that I had but a brief interlude in which I might avoid the same fate.

Sidling down the central aisle, carrying my Gladstone bag before me, I attempted to leave the dining car in as casual a mode as I could affect – trying to act as if I had merely left something in my compartment and I was sauntering back to claim it, before returning to take my breakfast like any other gentleman.

I didn't have a plan other than to try and improvise my way out of a tight spot. The corridor beyond the dining car was even more opulent than the carriage from which I had come. There was a heavy carpet on the floor, patterned in differing shades of dark red. Its thick pile lapped against the polished walnut-panelled walls. There were inlaid lines of fine gold and the ceiling was hung at regular intervals with miniature chandeliers fashioned from crystal glass. They sparkled in the bright sunlight that flickered in and out of the corridor as the train picked up speed. As I walked I passed, on my right, an occasional door. Each was numbered, also in inlaid gold, like a hotel chamber. There were only three doors. Numbers one and two were firmly closed, but number three was open, or at least partly so. As I passed I could see a man stretched out on a small divan. He glanced up idly at me, though with no particular interest. The chamber he occupied was more like a room than a train compartment. It occurred to me that this carriage was something more exclusive than the ordinary first class, having the appearance of a private saloon car. This impression was confirmed when I was unable to find any bathroom, even beyond the next vestibule. All such arrangements were clearly contained within each of the individual quarters. Any hope of secreting myself until the first appointed stop was quickly evaporating. Having reached the end of the car – where I was faced with a locked door of polished oak – I begin to feel decidedly panicked. Looked at coolly from this distance it seems like a matter of very little consequence. I had only to plead ignorance in as contrite a manner as possible and beg the indulgence of the guards until the first station – which couldn't be very far – but somehow, within that grand and private setting, the circumstances felt grave indeed. It was as if my trespass were breaking some deeply entrenched code of behaviour. I walked back and forth avoiding the dining car, not knowing how to proceed. I suppose I was waiting to be accosted and as such I wished the guards would speed towards me – though I had not the courage to give myself up. On maybe my third or fourth trip down the corridor I was startled by a call from the door of the open chamber – chamber number three.

'Hoy!' A face appeared at the door. A friendly face, not much older than mine. The man's hair was already thinning, however, creating the odd sense that his pate was ageing at a different rate from his features. 'That's the third time you've walked past in as many minutes,' he said. 'Can I be of help? Are you looking for someone?' I glanced up, back in the direction of the dining car and saw, moving down the corridor towards us, the first of the zealous guards.

'I'm terribly sorry,' I said unable to disguise my agitation. 'I seem to have made an awful mistake. I'm not supposed to be here.' He looked at me with unusually keen brown, almost black eyes. He had an avian appearance, not in any pinched or off-putting way, rather in the manner of something chimerical. For a moment I had the bizarre impression of him costumed at some masked ball – with the body of a man and the head of a bird. He had clearly sized up my situation very quickly and he smiled broadly. The bird-like impression fell away.

'Come on. Come in. You can be my guest. It's an awfully long journey to be travelling alone anyway.' He reached out with a black-gloved hand in order to take my Gladstone bag. With one more glance over my shoulder I entered his room.

'You can shut the door, if you like. I was only being lazy.' I did so and observed the smoothness with which the mechanism of the lock slid into its strike. 'Take a seat,' he said. 'I was just going to stoke the fire. We can order tea. Have you eaten?' He squatted down on his haunches before a small hearth and mantel built into the inner wall of the room. The sun was bright, flickering with our passage, making a zoetrope of the large picture windows. He struggled with a shovel full of coke, trying not to drop any as he moved it towards the fireplace, the task made difficult by the pitch and yaw of the train. As he tended to the fire, jabbing it uncertainly with a small iron poker, I looked around the immaculate room. Although I had been invited in I still felt tainted with criminality. I didn't want to compound this by being caught staring at his luxurious environs like some half-starved street urchin. The walls were the same polished walnut as the corridor, but they were augmented with fine marquetry comprised of many different hardwood veneers. The furniture (a small dining table, a bureau, a bookcase) was three-quarter sized – which created quite an unusual sensation. Indeed perched on the divan I felt like Alice on one of her adventures with the room shrinking around her. Behind me was a white-painted door, fractionally open, allowing a glimpse of a tiled space beyond – this must have been my saviour's bathroom. The fittings and upholstery were all exquisite: shot silk lampshades, thick velvet curtains. King George himself could have sat quite easily in here. On the wall in front of me was a large framed depiction of General Gordon's last stand. Directly opposite on the wall behind was another more formal portrait – whose subject I didn't recognise. It was as I was studying this, my neck twisted awkwardly, that my companion must have turned his attentions from the fire.

'You're admiring my paintings, I see.' He dusted the remnants of the coke from his gloves and sat in a dining chair opposite me. He was slightly too large for it, but did his best to disguise any discomfort this caused him.

'Please, you take the divan,' I said. 'Let me perch on a chair.'

'Nonsense. I'm fine. It is a pleasure to share one's comforts. I'm being terribly, terribly rude. Marr. Rupert James Elias.' He held out his hand to shake, though without removing his glove. It was only as I went to take it that I realised it was his left hand. I swapped my right for my own left, but mistimed the move making the handshake, when it came, fumbled and awkward.

'Consett. Robert. Malachi.' I uttered my middle name with the usual discomfort associated with its revelation, feeling I had no choice but to offer it since my companion had given his. We both returned to our seats eager to re-establish some kind of ease.

'Henry Ward Beecher,' said Marr. For a moment I didn't know to whom he was referring. He smiled, seeing this. 'The painting.' He gestured towards it with a movement of his eyes.

'I knew the other. General Gordon,' I said. 'I've seen it before.'

'These rooms are on long lease from the railway company. We are allowed to decorate them as we see fit.'

'You make this journey often, then,' I said. Feeling ridiculous in my coat and hat, given that the fire was now burning cheerfully, I removed both.

'My business takes me between London and Scotland. The company I work for has a number of mines throughout the region.'

'Coal?' I wondered what he did. He looked younger than me yet had the air in talking of his business as if he had been doing it all his life.

'Metals,' he said. 'Silver, copper, cobalt.'

'I know this painting,' I said, pointing to the depiction of Gordon's most desperate hour. 'It tells a remarkable story.'

'A fellow admirer?' He raised his eyebrows.

'Some say Gordon's behaviour was reckless – wilful even. To me his refusal to give way to the Mahdi was a rejection of fear and superstition. That the Mahdists severed his head and took it as a trophy tells us, quite concisely, everything we need know about them and everything we need know about us.'

'Assuming it is true. That this was his ultimate fate.'

'It is true,' I said.

He nodded at this.

'But the other portrait,' I said. 'The name is familiar.'

'The great supporter of the Union in the American Civil War. A passionate adversary of slavery – a fierce defender of women's suffrage and of Darwin's theory of evolution.'

'Of course. I did not recognise the face.' I studied the picture for a moment. 'It looks strong yet kind.' Marr nodded again. 'You are a fellow progressive,' I said, posing this as a statement rather than a question.

'Beecher's mission was to reform Christianity, not to destroy it,' he said, suddenly bristling. I was a little taken aback. I responded with a curt nod of my own, thinking it best to avoid this line of conversation if it was going to bring us into conflict. I had warmed to these surroundings already and did not much fancy giving them up having just stumbled upon them so providentially.

'It is cold today. Unexpectedly so given the brightness of the sunshine,' I said with as much good humour as I could produce.

He looked at me, his gaze alert and intense. 'I didn't mean to snap,' he said. 'You must forgive me, Mr Consett.' I waved away his apology as if the behaviour to which it referred were inconsequential. 'And please, tell me, where is it you are heading – and what makes you take the journey?'

For a moment I found myself wanting to answer the latter question with 'my father', which was strange because it had never occurred to me that that was the answer at all.

'I'm heading for London – and like yourself it is a matter of employment – except for me it is the beginning of something. An interview for a position in the civil service.'

'You wish to work in Government?'

'Indeed. If one is able to serve in any way at all – if one is called to do so – one has a duty to abide by that call.'

'Is that where your loyalty lies? With your country?'

A curious question, I thought, but answered it anyway. 'My country, of course.'

'And what is the nature of the position you are to take up? If you are successful in obtaining this position.'

'That, I'm afraid, is something I'm not at liberty to reveal, suffice to say that it involves the highest interest of the nation. And the Crown.'

'Goodness. It sounds fascinating.'

Tea arrived, together with a breakfast platter. Marr was most gracious in behaving as if my presence as his guest were a matter of pre-ordainment. He demanded another plate of breakfast and an extra cup and was most insistent that the same mistake not be made when it came to the lunch arrangement. He seemed to have some difficulty in pouring the teapot when the extra crockery arrived (which it did with notable promptness) so I took over the duties, and was as effusive as I could be in thanking him for his kindness and his largesse. After our affable beginning we seemed to have veered off to a less agreeable place and I was keen to manoeuvre us back to friendlier ground.

I don't know how long we had been travelling for or quite where we had got to on our journey when the train began to slow. We had stopped two or three times already – not that I paid any great attention to the stations' names. Berwick-upon-Tweed was among them, and Alnwick. I was aware that we had begun to head inland because the occasional flashes of grimy-looking ocean ceased, to be replaced with bare moorland, unbroken by tree, hedge or lane.

'The route is peculiar to this train,' said Marr buttering the last piece of toast. He offered it to me but I declined. 'It lengthens the journey but adds to the interest of what lies beyond the windows.' We had been speaking of Captain Scott. Marr had not heard the bad news and though not a passionate follower like myself he was distressed. 'A grim way to go,' he had said. 'But maybe there is something perversely comforting about being taken by the cold. There is a cleanness to it.'

'The discomfort would have been nothing to him – or to any of the party. I can imagine the failure wounding more,' was my response.

'Do you think he was open to the concept of hubris – was there a lack of humility in their venture?'

'There was courage in it. And there is nothing nobler.'

'Doesn't it take great courage to humble one's self? Is courage not a component of humility?'

'Now you sound like a philosopher. Debating the existence of chairs and tables.' The remark had intended to be light-hearted but Marr had gone notably silent. He was an odd creature. But kind – a point underlined by the offer of the last piece of toast.

It was now clear why the train had slowed so. We had come to the edge of a great curving embankment and the track began to arc, almost in the form of a semicircle, doubling back on itself. Huge cliffs of grassy moor towered on either side. A shadow engulfed the formerly bright compartment and we fell silent, listening to the rock and creak of the carriage. Then, unexpectedly, the escarpment dropped off on one side revealing a kind of low valley beyond. It was drear and bleak, beneath a silk-grey sky. Just visible some way around the semicircle was a large stone-built house and garden. It was hard to imagine a more unlikely setting, as it backed right on to the railway. We drew closer and the scale of the house became more apparent. It had extensive grounds spreading away in front of it, laid out in a series of terraces. Even from this distance it was clear that they had been unattended for some time, overgrown and wild in places, bare and scrubby-looking in others. There must have been some kind of driveway that led to a road, but it was no longer discernible, presumably hidden under the layers of bracken and dogwood that were flourishing at the edge of the property. The air here seemed very different – still and damp. There was a heaviness no doubt brought about by the enclosed nature of the surrounding geography. Who would have thought to build a house in such a location and why they would do so were the inevitable questions that came to mind.

I thought we were coming to a complete halt. This didn't actually occur, but we began to move so slowly that it felt inevitable. I assumed that the sharp curvature of the track at this point made the deceleration a necessity. It was such a dramatic bend that by the time we had completed going around it, we must have been travelling in the opposite direction from which we had come. When the train was at its slowest our compartment reached a point where we were almost parallel with the rear of the house. It was only then that I became aware of the huge graffito letters painted in an arching formation from its bottom left-hand corner reaching up to the top of the third floor and down again to the bottom right. Each letter must have been nearly two metres high. The overall impression was distinctly striking. The phrase it spelled out was arresting in its simplicity: 'God is love'.

It was natural enough as our train moved past to find one's head turning, to keep the extraordinary sight in view for as long as possible. Eventually the train rolled away from the curious embankment, the slopes of which fell sharply to be replaced by more conventional landscape of scrubby heathland dotted with twisted trees. The house disappeared from view and was no longer visible from the vantage point of the carriage window. Indeed if one had been in a soporific mood one could quite easily believe that the entire view had been dreamed. Neither myself nor Marr had spoken a word from the moment we had approached the house. It was only now that we were away from it that the silence ended.

Bound South

'You have not made this journey before, have you?' Marr was on his knees again before the fire, stoking it with his good hand, i.e. his left one. He poked and stirred with some force, as if eager to kindle the coals into new life. The temperature seemed to have dropped sharply. The brief period away from the winter sunlight had doubtless brought this about. 'You will not be familiar with the unusual sight of that derelict house.'

'Indeed. It was most unusual,' I said. He did not turn, but carried on attacking the hearth.

'Therefore you will not know any of the stories associated with it.'

'I've never heard tell of it. It is not the kind of place one is likely to forget.'

Marr was upright now, the fire glowing afresh. His gloved hands batted the coal-dust from his knees and he sat in the dining chair, angling it towards the heat.

'One story in particular is of interest,' he said. 'If you would like to hear it . . .'

I was not sure if I wanted to know more about the house or not, but it seemed rude to say no, given my position. Normally I enjoy a tale as much as the next chap, but something about the place's dark aspect made one shudder a little.

'Very much,' I said. 'If it throws light on the curious impression the place created.' I settled back on to the divan trying to make myself as comfortable as possible. Marr took a long breath, exhaled slowly and adjusted himself in his less than comfortable dining chair.

'The house was owned by a singular man who had led an uncommonly eventful life for one of his calling. He was a chaplain by vocation and had for many years been attached to St George's School in Sedgefield – which in former times had a more exalted reputation than it enjoys today. He married relatively late in life. There was a hint of impropriety about the affair – his wife being a much younger woman – that led the chaplain to leave the school and seek employment elsewhere. An unusual position came up: chaplain at a gold mine in South Africa.'

'Chaplain at a gold mine?' I said, not meaning to interrupt Marr so early in his tale – but it was such a curious point it felt like it needed qualification.

'Oh yes. It is more common than one might think – particularly abroad and in the Catholic countries. Mines are dangerous places, as I can attest, with many fatalities. A chaplain is a source of comfort among a God-fearing work force. The mine was in the De Kaap valley in the Eastern Transvaal and though the chaplain had never been out of the country before he took his young wife and in a spirit of bold adventure that perhaps you might appreciate, Mr Consett, he left these shores and embarked upon his new life.

'All went well for the first few years. The chaplain's form of simple solid religion honed over year after year of receptive schoolchildren was perfect for the ranks of uncomplicated mineworkers. Thinking they could not have children, the couple adopted two boys, orphaned by illness, though shortly after this the wife fell pregnant. Finding himself with a young family this new rugged life brought many discomforts, particularly for the mother of his child, but there were compensations too. In fact his wife took up metalworking and became quite adept at it, fashioning crucifixes and christening brooches, which she forged in her own little crucible. However, it was around this time, when the chaplain was feeling most settled and most happy – if happy is a word that could ever attach itself to him – that his fortunes underwent an unfavourable turn. The mine and its surrounding enclave were subject to occasional raids by gangs of roaming outlaws known as *Kwaimans* – a combination of bush men and Boer fighters who had turned rogue – 'gone native' is the expression often used today. The raids were resisted with arms and were not usually bloody affairs, however on this occasion several men were killed and the chaplain's young wife was taken by the raiding party, disappearing with them into the bush.

Search parties were sent out and the army was brought in to assist but it was all to no avail. The wife was found neither alive nor dead, there was no sign of the raiding party and she was assigned the status of another victim of the African frontier. The chaplain was desolate, unable to control his grief. The mining company – which was adequately insured for such eventualities – thought the best course to pay the man off, which it did with a considerable amount of pure gold.'

Marr paused in his tale and rolled up his left sleeve, baring the flesh of his forearm. He pressed it against the side of the tea-pot to check if there was any heat left in it. He pushed the service bell, then settled back into his chair, rolling down his sleeve.

'Now a wealthy man the chaplain returned to England, to the portion of the country he was most familiar with. He had no connections here, other than historical, but clearly he felt some affection for the place, or maybe it had a sense of security about it. Or perhaps it was all he knew to do, somewhere familiar to go while he recovered from his wounds. The house was for sale and he bought it. Whether it was all that was on the market in the area at that time or whether its peculiar aspect suited the tenor of his emotions it is hard to know. Whatever, he cannot have been thinking of his children – so recently deprived of a mother – for they would surely not benefit from its isolated environs.

'Time passed, the chaplain became older and more anxious, unwilling to let the children out of his sight. It was this that led him to employ a governess to oversee their education rather than send them away for their schooling. Naturally, the children began to resent the feeling of being held hostage by the situation and a level of habitual disobedience led to a variety of different governesses making their way to and from the dark house by the railway. It was the daughter, however, who perceived most clearly that the real source of their misery lay in the souring heart of their now-distant father. Oh, he was not distant in proximity, for he prowled around the corridors and rooms like a watchful jailer, keeping his attention fixed on everything that transpired between the children and their instructor. But at his core he was dried up, like a diseased tree whose twisted branches can no longer bear any fruit at all. He could not resolve his grief, unable or unwilling to reach the shores that lay at its furthest edge. Every time they came into view he chose to turn himself around and set sail again on those black waters. And now he was lost to them – until death came to take him to the greater abyss beyond.

'His daughter was a sharp girl, at least as sharp as her father, and she saw the poison in him. By the time she was thirteen, he had become the enemy. It is perhaps unfortunate that at this point fate intervened in two separate but opposing ways. Firstly, the latest governess to be appointed was quite different from any of her predecessors. She was a modern-thinking, university-educated young woman, an aspiring writer who had published several political pamphlets and had read – and understood – the best of the nineteenth-century European thinkers: Hegel, Schopenhauer, James. It is unlikely the chaplain was aware of this – unlikely she would have made him aware of it given that she needed the employment, but in the chaplain's daughter she recognised a kinship and thus set about providing her with a bespoke education. And the young girl prospered. Simultaneously the chaplain fell under a quite different influence. He had been reading collections of the speeches of William Jennings Bryan – the American Presbyterian politician who was, and still is, of course, a great advocate of religious conservatism and opponent of the writings of Charles Darwin. Whether the daughter knew of this or whether what follows is coincidental it is hard to say, but the governess had just completed teaching Darwin's theories and the young girl was much taken with them. Of her own volition she read not just *On The Origin of Species*, but *The Descent of Man* and also *The Expression of Emotions in Man and Animals*. She was gripped by these works and developed a deep and personal connection to them. It may be that she saw in them a means to combat her father and his increasingly oppressive and conservative religious views. The attack began slowly and insidiously – chance remarks made at the dinner table about biblical inerrancy. There was an element of mischief to these comments, which the chaplain, though not possessed of what one might describe as a sense of humour, took in that spirit and let pass. But then the young girl's comments became more specific. The chaplain was a wily man. He was not an intellectual or an academic, but he was clever. Nor was he easily provoked. It's possible that there was a component of this debate that he relished. Almost daily the volume of remarks and queries increased. One day the daughter pointed out that Isaiah's claim that 'the moon has a light of its own' was inaccurate. We now know that the moon has no light, it merely reflects what comes from the sun – the true light of our solar system, she pointed out. Patiently the chaplain countered, saying that while this may be true from a scientific perspective, on a practical level the moon is indeed a source of light, with a particular character of its own and if she doubts this she should go outside on an unclear night and observe what happens when the moon is revealed from behind an obscuring cloud. The next day the daughter said she had been reading the Book of Jonah and it stated that the city of Nineveh was so large that it took three days to cross. By her sum this must make it over sixty miles wide, larger than any city now known to man, when the earth's population is immensely greater than it would have been in these times. The chaplain pointed out that this objection was dependent upon her reading of how long a city took to cross. Jonah may well have stopped many times on his way in order to give account of his mission, or for many more mundane reasons. The time it took him to do so could not be used as a strict measure of distance. From here the daughter leaped to the New Testament. She said both Matthew and Luke claimed that Satan showed Jesus a mountain from which he could see all the kingdoms of the world. And now she was adamant. No such mountain could exist for the world is irrefutably a globe. The chaplain explained, once again with seemingly infinite patience, that it was her reading which was in error rather than the text itself. She was not taking into account Satan's wiles and treacherous facilities. It was entirely within his power to create a false image in the Christ's mind for diabolic ends, and this is indeed what both Matthew and Luke were describing. The daughter was unbowed. She now seemed to turn all her attention to the Book of Genesis. The girl had inherited her father's cunning and everything thus far was a preamble designed to lead in to her main point of attack. Her next question was innocuous enough. She explained that she was puzzling over a sentence in Genesis that said snakes eat dust. This cannot be true, she was sure, because there is no sustenance in such a diet and the animals would die. The chaplain explained with his customary patience that the good book is merely pointing out the true nature of the venomous creature, and the fact that as it is a low crawling thing it cannot help but ingest dirt and dust with every mouthful. The daughter nodded and accepted this, but she was back again the following day with a more pointed question. She had read in Genesis Chapter 30 how cattle can be made to produce striped offspring if they are exposed to striped poles when breeding. She found this claim to be extraordinary and she was keen to hear her father's clarification – which she was sure would be as excellent and inarguable as usual. It was the first time that the chaplain seemed both lost and angry. He worked to control his anger. He strove to sound as reasoned and unshaken as always. He was aware of the passage to which his daughter referred and that this was an example of God's power. There are occasions when God intervenes in human affairs for his own reasons, as he did here to assist Jacob, he said. No other explanation is necessary. The daughter wanted to know what scientific process God made use of to create stripes on the cattle. The chaplain referred her firmly to the answer he had just given. The next day her question was again about Genesis. This time she wanted to know about Noah's Ark. She had been pondering over the dimensions described in Genesis – three hundred by fifty cubits, a cubit being the length of an average man's forearm. Admittedly this made for a large vessel, comparable with a modern ocean steamer, but even so, if one thinks of the innumerate species that science has already classified, it becomes difficult to conceive how two of every such creature should be contained, particularly the animals who were not native to Palestine of the thirtieth century BC. She wondered how Noah was able to find a polar bear or other creatures of the Antarctic for example, or creatures native to the Americas, a continent not yet discovered by outsiders which presumably was to be covered with flood-waters as well since the indigenous men that were there were wicked too. The chaplain now bristled at his daughter's provocation. With less good humour or patience than he had responded to previous questions he told her firmly that she was underestimating the volume of Noah's vessel, that she was mistakenly thinking that two of every animal included aquatic creatures who hardly needed saving from their environments. That many of the species she referred to as being innumerate were in fact tiny – insects and invertebrates – thousands of which could be stored in a plain chest of drawers if it were suitably prepared, and that she needed to think more clearly before mocking the revealed word of God. Perhaps a wiser, more temperate personality would have ceased these questions having reached this point. The slow stoking of the chaplain's anger had fired an engine within him that was not about to shut itself off. But the daughter was not temperate and she was fighting her own battle for survival, though she may not have put it in such a way to herself. So the following morning's breakfast was witness to another question – the one that directly precipitated the terrible events that were to follow it.

The daughter, very clearly, in an articulate manner that belied her years, wanted to know if her father was familiar with the writings of Mr Darwin, which had established themselves in recent years as scientific fact. For the first time in this series of questions, the chaplain did not respond directly. Whether or not he knew that this is where these morning exchanges had been leading, or whether it was something that only became apparent in that moment, we cannot say, but his daughter could not have selected a more raw or inflammatory spot on which to apply pressure. Fresh from Mr Bryan's pamphlets and incensed that the simple faith on which he had structured his own life was now being so challenged, the chaplain was unable to frame a response. Oblivious to this, or because of it, the daughter pushed on. The Bible, she said, states unequivocally that creation was completed in six days and yet Mr Darwin's studies have revealed that species have evolved and differentiated over time – incrementally from generation to generation – through a self-governing dumb, mute process of trial and error. How can one position possibly be reconciled to the other? There was a long and terrible silence that evoked the very void itself. And then, with a roar of primal rage, the chaplain placed his hands under the rim of the heavy oak table upon which they dined and upended it – pushing it towards his daughter. She managed to move out of the way in time to avoid being injured, as she would have been had the table caught her. The chaplain advanced upon her and hauled her upstairs, carrying her under his arm like a mess of laundry. She struggled but he was determined. He dragged her to the top of the house, to the attic room that overlooked the railway tracks, and threw her inside, bolting the door. He stormed downstairs and dismissed the governess that instant, insisting that she be out of the house within the half-hour. She demanded a car be ordered for her. But he became so fierce in his response that the woman packed her possessions and fled in a shorter time than he had commanded. The rage now burning inside the chaplain had released something within him – a fierce satanic power that drove him to stalk the narrow corridors of his fiefdom. His daughter had spent some time clamouring for her release, but eventually she desisted. She waited to see what her father's next move would be. The house was silent for the rest of the day. The daughter remained quietly in her impromptu prison – disturbed only by the shake of the occasional trains as they passed. In the middle of the afternoon there was a sudden flurry of action. The father opened the door and brought in a jug of water and a small bucket. And then he explained his position. He realised he had been derelict in his duty towards his only daughter – by delegating her moral education to another woman he had brought this state of affairs on himself. He would have to work fast to expel the poison this governess had introduced into his child's soul. She needed to begin by being penitent – asking him – and through him God Himself – for forgiveness. The daughter stared at him. She had had a long time to think and this command was hardly a surprise to her. She had already resolved to resist her father's demands – and the mulish determination that was part of his character was at least as strong in her. For something had been ignited in her too, a fire that warmed her as no other had done: the fire of truth and the freedom that it brought. The irony was not lost on her that the Bible itself made the same observation – that the truth would set her free. She made it clear that it would not be possible for her to retract anything or beg any forgiveness, because the sin was to *not* ask the questions. She had been doing as she was made to do. The chaplain nodded. He too had thought ahead and this response was not unanticipated. He had a task for her. She may think he was an ill-educated fool, a country-reared dullard of little imagination – but this was not an accurate estimate. He had some learning in him too. He had written out, on foolscap paper a certain argument – a logical proof of God's existence formulated by St Anselm in the eleventh century. The greatest philosophers and logicians had wrestled ever since with Anselm's premises and conclusion but none had been able to find a flaw in the argument, or successfully contest it in any satisfactory way. The chaplain had laid out the line of reasoning clearly for his daughter. And now she had a choice. She could accept Anselm's proposition and show faith, humility and fear to her Creator, while praying for her forgiveness – or she could counter Anselm's argument, and find a flaw in it. Either of these outcomes would secure her food and water, and indeed release from her attic prison. But nothing else would. He handed his daughter the paper, left the room and then shut the door.

'There was no response for at least an hour, nearer two. And then the chaplain heard his daughter calling to him. Surprised at this rapid turnaround he raced to the top of the house. But, it transpired, she only wanted a pencil, and some more paper. He granted her request.'

Marr sat up and stretched. 'I fancy some tea,' he said. 'Do you fancy some more tea?'

'I do, yes,' I said. 'But you can't break off the story here. I need to find out what became of the girl.' The world beyond the carriage had darkened considerably. Marr reached behind him and flicked a switch turning on the electric light above him.

'Cold again,' he said, and was down on his knees once more before the fire. He poured a stream of coke from the scuttle into the hearth making burning hot embers fly into the air around him. For a moment he was surrounded by a little halo of glowing gold. He turned, blinking his eyes. 'Before I continue,' he said, still on his knees before me, 'I need to fill you in on the basics of Anselm's argument – unless you are already familiar with it?'

I shook my head, for I wasn't. 'Modern languages,' I said. 'Not classics.'

'I trained as an engineer – but the argument is simple

enough to grasp, which is why, no doubt, it has endured all these centuries.' I looked at him blankly so he added, 'And you need to have it in mind, in order to understand what follows.'

'Who was Anselm?' I said unafraid at showing my own ignorance on ecclesiastical matters – in fact the reverse was true. I was proud of it.

'One of the most interesting Archbishops of Canterbury. He objected to the Crusades – on moral grounds. Though none of this is necessary knowledge. The argument is quite self-sustaining.'

I nodded, hoping that I would not be lost in some impenetrable philosophy.

'Anselm's argument is an a priori proof of God's existence. It is derived entirely from reason itself.'

'I see,' I said, already feeling lost.

'Honestly, there's nothing to it. And yet it is strangely slippery. It does indeed do what it sets out to do – which is provide a self-contained logical proof of God's existence – but it does so in a kind of fox-like way. You hear it and think there must be some catch. But the queer thing is that, as the chaplain explained to his daughter, it has defied the best efforts of logicians and philosophers to find the flaw in it for nearly a thousand years. The argument goes something like this – to begin we need a definition of God and Anselm proposes "a being than which nothing greater can be thought of or conceived". Would you agree with that as a place to start?' Already this open talk of matters divine was making me uncomfortable as it reminded me of my own father, though he would never have approached the subject from this direction (or indeed from the chaplain's direction either).

'I can see that it would serve as a place to begin. If you have to think of a God at all,' I said.

'Very good, very good,' said Marr. 'Then we can proceed to the next premise.' Already I was bridling, however. Something in me didn't want to concede even this much.

'Actually, hold on a moment, Marr,' I said. 'Does this really function as a definition? Isn't it a bit arbitrary? Wouldn't you be better off with "God is the ultimate being" or "God is the ruler of the Universe", or something?'

'Well, my friend,' said Marr – as if he had been faced with these objections before – 'I think you'll find that this is what old Anselm had in mind. "The greatest being one could possibly think of" encompasses both of the statements you've just made. Anselm was looking to sum up something essential in his first premise – something that incorporates all other possible definitions – hence the rather generalised language.' I made a gesture indicating I would concede the objection. 'Very well,' said Marr, looking pleased. 'So we come to Anselm's second premise. He proposes that it is greater for something to exist in reality than purely in the mental realm. Before you object to this one let me illustrate the point. If there are two things – an imaginary hundred guineas the thought of which you are holding in your head and a real pile of a hundred guineas in individual notes – which is the greater?'

'What do you mean by greater?' I said, even more wary.

'Well – which could achieve things, do more for you, the merely thought of thing or its real counterpart?'

'The answer is obvious,' I said, gaining a scent of where this was going and not liking it.

'And another illustration, even more pertinent to young bachelors such as ourselves – if you have in your head the thought of a beautiful, enchanting young woman, delightful as company, fair in face and especially in figure' – Marr raised his eyebrows and I found myself smiling – 'and also the real woman – beautiful, elegant and even more enchanting in actuality – which of those would you consider greater?'

'You already know the answer,' I said, still smiling.

'Then you'll agree that Anselm's point is well made?'

'I will concede that point to him and to you,' I said.

'Very good. Very good. So to the third premise: if the being about which nothing greater can be thought were to exist *only* in the mental realm it would be possible to think of something greater – namely the same thing existing in actuality – and that this then implies that the being you were first thinking of is not a being about which nothing greater can be thought to exist, because you have just thought of something greater – the one that exists in reality.' He looked at me with some zeal in his eyes.

'Yes,' I said. 'I can just about grasp that on purely logical terms.'

'Well, then,' said Marr, 'the being other than which nothing greater can be thought or conceived cannot exist only in the mental realm – it must also exist in reality because otherwise it is not the being other than which nothing greater can be thought of or conceived. This is Anselm's conclusion.' He sat back, satisfied with his expounding of the old saint's argument.

I stared at him for some time, trying to go over the thing in my head. The problem was – paradoxically – that it was simple to grasp, the logic of it too. And though it felt that there was a cheat somewhere in its spare and plain premises it was very hard to pin it down. One assumed that it must lie in the definition laid out in the first premise but when one went backwards mentally and examined it in isolation it seemed at least acceptable within the context of the argument. But then, if one did accept it, it was hard then to find a chink one could exploit to counter in the subsequent premises and – to me – unacceptable conclusion. I kept finding myself starting sentences 'But . . .' then immediately trailing off with Marr smiling at me in a slightly smug and insufferable manner.

'I know what you are thinking and what it feels like – but it's no good. The argument does not crumble so easily.'

'Then it is not an argument,' I said. 'For in merely linguistic or logistic terms it may satisfy, but in one's bones it does not. Indeed on that level it feels empty and specious –

nothing more than a piece of parlour trickery. And who could be satisfied with that? Who could build their faith and belief on such a thing?' I sat back on the divan, feeling my heartbeat pulsing in my neck. Marr's silly logic – or Anselm's, if it was really his – had angered me acutely.

'Well – that may be – but we are losing ourselves. I am in the process of telling you a story, and in this story the chaplain is using Anselm's argument to make a point to his daughter – not just to make a point, but to subjugate her to his will.'

I tried to calm myself. I was aware that – for a moment at least – I had taken Marr's account as a personal affront. 'I'm sorry,' I said. 'Forgive my ill tempered objections – please continue.' Marr acknowledged my apology with a nod and settled back into his seat.

'So, let us remind ourselves that the chaplain's daughter is imprisoned in the attic room, with Anselm's argument written out on foolscap paper by her father. She has been left with the instruction that either she accepts the conclusion of the argument and prostrates herself before her father's will or she finds a way of refuting it. Her father has made it clear to her that she will receive no food or water until she provides him with her definitive response. Naturally he expected her to capitulate rapidly before such unassailable logic. But he underestimated his daughter. Considerably.

'Sat there alone in the bare, cold, wood-floored room she pondered on what to do next. She could not swallow down or contain the newly found spirit of freedom that had been the governess's gift to her, certainly not to please her father – who she may once have felt love for, as a small child, but who had receded from her with each passing year since the disappearance of her mother. So she did something that per-haps one might have thought anathema to her. She closed her eyes, breathed deeply and she prayed. Not to the god of her father but to something else – to the spirit that flared inside her and she felt so acutely, like a spectral light in the dusty gloom of the bare-walled prison. She prayed for some time – until the answer became clear to her. When it came it surprised her. But she could not argue with it. It told her to set to work.

'The first night passed, and then the second day. The chaplain did not go to his daughter. He was determined not even to give her that. He had decided it was essential that she realised her sin herself and took a complete responsibility for her own atonement. Night after night, no hint of repentance came forth from the barred door. Only the faint sound of scribbling and the rustling of paper. Finally on the fifth morning the two brothers, who had walked in greater fear of their father than their sister did, resolved that something must be done. Their father was unreachably locked in his study, his *pater familias* Bible open on his knees, rocking back and forth in furious prayer. The boys crept to the top of the house and mustering all their strength they forced open the door of the impromptu prison. Eventually the heavy wood splintered and cracked. And they had arrived in fortunate time. For their sibling lay sprawled among sheafs of scribbled-on paper, on the edge of consciousness. In her hand she clutched three pieces of neatly-written foolscap. She would not let them go. It was only when her father appeared, drawn by the commotion he had heard from two floors below, that she released them, into his trembling hands.

'What she had written went something like this:

I have thought for an extended period on this matter and have carefully considered it from every position as I have been taught to do by Miss Millican. I have reached a definitive conclusion – St Anselm's argument is fatally flawed. This is a record of how I got to it.

It seems clear to me that Anselm's argument can be expressed in the following form:

Firstly, it is possible to speak of something-than-which-nothing-greater-can-be-thought. The phrase does refer to a thing which exists in the mental realm at least, even if it has no correlative existing in reality.

Secondly, existence in reality is greater than existence in the mental realm. I understand this and accept it as a concept. We can say if something-than-which-nothing-greater-can-be-thought were to exist only in the mind, it would be possible to think of something greater, namely the same thing existing in reality. (I can illustrate this point to myself in the following manner: a real prime minister of England is greater than an imaginary one – because he has intelligence and considerable power and through the use of these faculties he is capable of exerting notable effects throughout the world for the general good. None of this could be said of a purely imaginary prime minister. Hence the existing prime minister is greater than the one who exists only in the mind.)

Thirdly, this last premise implies that something-than-which-nothing-greater-can-be-thought is not after all something-than-which-nothing-greater-can-be-thought if it is only in the mind – why? Because it can always be trumped by a corresponding version of itself that has actual existence in reality.

Therefore, something-than-which-nothing-greater-can-be-thought cannot exist only in the mental realm, it has to exist also in reality – or it is not what it says it is.

It seems to me that the problematic area in all of the above is the formula St Anselm uses to define God – "something-than-which-nothing-greater-can-be-thought". It is not an unequivocally clear statement. It is in fact open to a number of various interpretations which cloud Anselm's reasoning.

Firstly, it could be interpreted thusly – "a nature which is so great that no nature that is greater can be thought of". Now this interpretation will not serve Anselm's purpose. Why? Because an atheist is bound to disagree with it. If this atheist is English and a patriot he is likely *to claim that under this interpretation Anselm's formula actually refers to the British Prime Minister not to God – for Mr Gladstone (as arguably the most powerful intelligent being in the Universe) may indeed in this sense be something-than-which-nothing-greater-can-be-thought. The believer will argue against this because he can think of something greater – namely God. But it is a simple matter for the atheist to counter this. He can say he considers the believer to be mistaken regarding the greatness of God because if one assumes God does not exist – God's nature cannot* in fact *be as great as Gladstone's since* real *existence is the most important criterion for greatness. The believer may argue that a God who exists would surely be greater than Gladstone. True, says the atheist, but if God does not* in fact *exist then the phrase "an existing God" does not identify anything real, therefore it does not identify a nature which is* in fact *greater than Mr Gladstone's.*

So the believer needs to come up with an interpretation of Anselm's formula which will guarantee that the thing it refers to is – irrefutably – at least as great as an existing God. Such an interpretation might be as follows – "a nature which is so great that no nature could conceivably be greater". On this reading something-than-which-nothing-greater-can-be-thought can only refer to an unsurpassably great nature. And yet the atheist can still object to this – for given his beliefs what could this nature be? It cannot be the nature of an existing God for that nature has no corresponding equivalent in reality and therefore does not fulfil the requirements of this interpretation of Anselm's formula. This is the crux of the matter. Unless we already know *that God exists, it is not possible to know that any nature is in actuality sufficiently great to satisfy this formula. For Anselm's argument to work the greatness of a nature must be a question of fact, not one of definition.*

Jeremy Dyson

So the believer may try a third interpretation of Anselm's God formula – something along the lines of "a nature which can be conceived to be so great that no nature could conceivably be greater". Well, this version does finally refer to a nature which we might recognise as being divine. For the properties usually attributed to Him – omnipotence, omniscience, moral perfection, etc. – are such that no other imaginable nature could be conceivably greater. The problem for the believer is that if he uses this interpretation of Anselm's formula in his argument, his argument fails. Why? Because it is not necessary for there to be a corresponding God in reality to make the statement and have it stand. In this interpretation – because he has been conceived to be so – God qualifies as something-than-which-nothing-greater-can be thought even if he doesn't in fact exist. The idea of Him alone is enough to fulfil things. Existence in reality is no longer a trump.

There is a fourth possible interpretation of the formula which invokes a greater level of necessity. It would go something like "a nature which necessarily has such a degree of greatness that no nature could conceivably be greater". Any nature to which this reading of the formula refers must be the nature of a necessarily existing God. But the atheist's refutation remains – that there is simply no such nature. The believer's claim is nothing but an unvalidated assertion. The existence of a real counterpart cannot simply be made true of a nature by definition alone. If there is no such being in fact *then this nature has no counterpart existing in reality, regardless of what is demanded by the definition.*

It is clear from all this that Anselm's argument is critically flawed. Of the four possible interpretations of his formula, only the third successfully refers to the nature of a supreme God, even in an atheistic Universe. But as we have seen for this very reason the subsequent argument fails to be valid. There is nothing more to be said.

'The chaplain – who had scanned the pages as he stood – with his daughter suffering beneath him, retired to his study, leaving the matter of the girl's care to his intervening sons. One could imagine it possible that he would just dismiss what she had written, regardless of its validity. But no. Some other battle was being waged here. And the rules of engagement – in the chaplain's mind at least – were clear. After many hours the silence in the house was rent by a ferocious scream. For it seemed, to his distress and disgust and by his own terms, his daughter's will had triumphed. Not just her will but her intellect. For a considerable time the only sound emerging from the study was that of a frantic pacing, followed by periods of silence. The hours became a day, and then two. Meanwhile the brothers nursed their sister – getting her to take some water and then some plain food. She could barely keep it within her, but they did what they could to bring comfort – difficult though it was in that increasingly benighted house. From beneath there came now the sound of activity. The chaplain had left his study. He seemed to be collecting items and equipment and installing himself in the basement. The first hint that the brothers had of what was afoot was a sense of rising heat in the house. There was a furnace in the cellar, capable of driving a hypocaustal central heating system, but the chaplain never lit it believing that to be too comfortable was to be in the province of Satan. Nevertheless stifling air now flowed out of the various vents and apertures distributed around the building to a degree not known by the children before. The whole atmosphere became heated like a hothouse at Kew. When they heard the chaplain climbing up the stairs they tried to bar the door from him for they feared what he was going to do to the girl, who was only just returning to a conscious and stable state. But the father was not to be denied. He opened the door with a single strike from his boot and strode inside, picking up the girl in one motion. She hung loose in his arms like an eiderdown. The sons – who normally went in terror of their parent and master – pleaded with him to leave the girl as she needed to recover. One of the boys tried weakly to wrestle with the chaplain but his efforts came to nothing. The man marched down the stairs transporting his daughter to her final cleansing lesson.

'It should be said at this point that when the chaplain had described himself as having some learning in him this was in fact quite true. It was mostly the learning of an autodidact – but a characteristic of this kind of education is its catholic breadth. And typically many unusual and esoteric facts and areas of knowledge are retained by a self-taught mind. If the chaplain had an area of specialism it was history, but not of the classical kind that one might pick up at university or school. He was fascinated by the history of what might be labelled ecclesiastical adventure – from the Crusades through to contemporary mission stations in Africa. None more gripped his imagination than the conquistadors of the sixteenth and early seventeenth centuries. Fragments of knowledge are apt to surface at the most unusual times and gripped as the chaplain was in his feverish contest with his own daughter, and his anger at her profound disobedience, one such item had bobbed into the forefront of his mind and it refused to sink. The second wave of Spanish invaders to arrive in the Americas were possessed of a more proselytising zeal than their predecessors. They had many weapons with which to fight the war against unbelief but one of the most cruel and feared was the practice of *obeisance* or obeyance. This pitiless technique sardonically used the Mayans' own adoration and near-idolatrous worship of gold itself against them. The recalcitrant native was strapped into a specially-adapted wicker chair, his bent knees exposed. An amount of gold was made molten in a crucible and it was poured on to the unfortunate savage's naked joints. It was allowed to sear for a period (the poor wretch's screams serving as an incentive for his brethren to convert) and then the legs were tempered with cold water. An amount of the metal would scorch its way deep into the joint. The unlucky devil was from then on forced to adopt a position of permanent penitence before the Christian God for as long as he continued to live. Now what vile perversity of spirit inculcated this idea into the chaplain's mind at this time we cannot know . . .'

Marr paused for a moment, perhaps searching for the right words for the abomination that I feared – correctly – he was going to describe.

'Were he here himself to justify his actions he would doubtless tell you it was God who gave the instruction. Perhaps it is possible he believed this. However he explained it to his own conscience, his anger found satisfaction in the idea. When the daughter arrived in the cellar, carried over her father's shoulder like a bale of cloth, she was surprised to see her mother's old crucible heating in the heart of the basement furnace, the few remaining nuggets of gold melting in the white heat. Her father had prepared a chair . . . I need not tell you what transpired other than the girl's screams were so loud and so terrible that they inspired her two brothers to take the most drastic action they could. Searching the house for whatever weapons were to be found – kitchen knives, garden implements – they broke down the door and confronted the insane chaplain. The room was full of smoke. The girl was bound weeping and shrieking in her chair. A terrible struggle ensued. Though neither brother shared a blood tie with the girl they fought like demons for her. The father did not survive.'

Marr was silhouetted against the window, a low red sun burning behind him. I could not see his face. The train rattled over a set of points, the solid-looking wooden floor shaking beneath us.

'What happened to the daughter?' I asked, bound uncritically in his story like a child.

'The brothers tried to nurse her – and they sought help from outside – but she died after some weeks from septicaemia. Already weakened by her semi-starvation she was unable to fight the infection.'

'And the dead father? The brothers?'

Marr shrugged his shoulders.

'But surely, such a case – the courts – the newspapers . . .'

Again he shrugged his shoulders. He looked away, out of the window at the setting sun.

'Shall we take lunch . . . ?' he said. 'Late for lunch, I know, but they will serve if I ask.' He turned back and smiled at me.

We ate the lunch, when it arrived, in relative silence. I could not help but be haunted by the narrative he had recounted. It was an extraordinary story – and it had succeeded in dissolving much of the journey for we were now not far from London – but I doubted its veracity. Marr was a gifted fabulist and an amateur philosopher – I had deduced that much already – but the more a story gripped and provoked, the less inclined I was to believe it to be true. He had by his own admission made the journey many times. Intrigued by the house he had spun his remarkable tale, honed it and refined it, and I was no doubt not the first audience to be entranced by it. In fact the more I thought about it, the more this explanation made sense. The keenness with which he had invited me within, just so he would be able to recount his tale when we had gone past the strange house by the tracks. I smiled at this thought.

'What's funny, old chap?' he said, waving the piece of cold chicken in his hand.

'Nothing.' I was not going to insult him by sharing my conclusion – not after his kindness to me, even if it was supported by an ulterior motive.

The train pulled through a thick fog that had begun several miles outside the city. It came into Euston almost exactly on time.

'I suppose this is where we part,' I said. I peered through the glass. Tendrils of mist reached into the station concourse itself. I buttoned my coat against the cold.

'Indeed,' was all Marr said. He had been quiet for the last

phase of the journey. I experienced a tinge of guilt, as if I had transgressed against him in some way, though I was sure I hadn't.

'Listen, old chap. I really am most grateful for what you did – helping me out of a scrape – and sharing . . . well, sharing everything with me. It was most kind of you. Most decent. If I should – secure my position – maybe we could meet again.'

'That would be capital,' he said. He reached for his travelling bag, which was on a parcel shelf above the divan. He struggled to grip it.

'Allow me,' I said, quickly stretching out, to prevent it from falling on him. I took the bag and moved it out towards the open door in the corridor across the car. I jumped down on to the platform, taking the bag with me and reached up for Marr, to help him disembark. He had removed his gloves. I took his right hand without thinking and immediately felt a shock – as if from a static charge. There were cold smooth patches among stiffer, scalier, warmer skin. As he joined me on the ground my gaze snapped to where we touched. I tried hard not to show any emotion at all. For the hand was scarred, injured in the most terrible but beautiful way. Swirls of livid pink scar tissue coiled round bright metal – pure spirals of burnished gold that seemed as much a part of Marr as the living flesh that surrounded them. My eyes moved quickly to his face. He returned my gaze. Momentarily I felt as if I were looking into his heart, and he into mine. I held his hand firmly – then released it. I found myself embracing him. I felt a corresponding pressure from him. I did not know what to say – and so said nothing. I don't know how much time passed. Eventually we let go of each other.

'Please take care of yourself,' I said.

'Yes,' he said simply. He put on his gloves and picked up his bag in his left hand. I watched him walk away, fading slowly into the encroaching mist. And then I set off myself –

towards Whitehall and an approaching war that would change my life, and the world too, in ways I could not possibly conceive.

But that, as they say, is another story.

Michael

It started with a Valentine's card.

Danny hated Valentine's day. At seventeen he had yet to receive a card, or indeed to send one. So on 11 February, walking back through town from college, Danny was surprised to find himself heading into Mathers in the Merrion Centre, facing the temporary lines of hearts and bunnies, the repeating pinks and reds. He reached out and picked up a glossy picture of Pooh Bear. He opened it. 'Roses are red, Eeyore is blue, Honey is sweet, says Winnie the Pooh'. He put it down again. It seemed juvenile and unappealing. He looked down the row, not knowing what he was searching for. He paused at a smaller card, more expensive. It featured a heart, like most of the others, but it was dark purple, almost blue – as if it was suffocating. There was no message inside. The design was stark and graphic.

Even as he left the shop with the card hidden away in his shoulder bag he didn't know what he was going to do with it, or why he had bought it. This was what he was like. His own actions were mysterious to him. He made himself feel sick.

Dinner was quiet. Or rather he was quiet. His brothers sat on either side, oblivious to him. Had he bought the card to impress them? Because by now he'd decided he was going to post it to himself. Who was it from? He would make up a name before he wrote it. He would disguise his

175

handwriting. Carefully. They would see it on Wednesday morning. He would open it, say nothing, put it in his bag, go to college.

He sat in his room with a candle burning, the door bolted. He'd put the fastening on himself two years ago – a bathroom lock he'd bought from Woolworths. He took a fine-nibbed Pilot pen from the wooden box on his bookcase. He wrote the card. 'To Daniel, from ?, with love . . .' He adopted a careful, ornamental style – almost like calligraphy. He added a single kiss. He let the ink dry and closed the card, then replicated the hand on the light-brown paper envelope, this time using his full name – Daniel MacFadden – followed by his address. He tried to imagine not knowing who he was as he wrote it out. He placed the card inside his bag, laying it flat along the bottom. Tomorrow he would buy a book of stamps.

If Danny had done things in the order that he'd planned them then what followed may never have occurred. As it was he didn't post the card. It lay, semi-forgotten, at the bottom of the bag, already a matter of some half-conscious shame. Maybe he had no intention of posting it after all. Another one of his opaque rituals that resisted comprehension. And then, during lunchtime sitting in the common room, Jardine and his crew were playing soccer with a tennis ball, rebounding it off the walls, scoring points when they hit pictures or windows. Danny sat in one corner by the folding doors, an uneaten sandwich on his lap. As he might have expected, the ball came close to him several times. Danny wasn't going to react, even when it flew by centimetres from his face. He would have succeeded in this aspiration had the ball not landed in his bag. It was Jardine himself who was responsible for the kick.

'Come on, Gollum – give it back.' At first Danny didn't even respond. 'Gollum, you dick,' said Jardine making his way over towards Danny. And as he arrived Danny remembered the card. Instinctively he pulled the bag – a dirty

Adidas holdall – on to his lap and zipped it closed. He should have taken the ball out first of course, but he didn't.

'Give it back, Pogle,' said Jardine, reaching for it with long arms. He had red hair and the colour of it seemed to blur into the acne on his face. Danny clutched the bag to himself. He couldn't let Jardine get hold of it.

'No,' he heard himself say.

Jardine laughed. Pickering and Whieldon, his cohorts, laughed too.

'Give it to me now, Gollum, or I'll fucking nut you. I'll fucking hurt you.'

'No,' said Danny. There was no courage in this. It was blind self-preservation. Because Jardine would see the card. He tried to resist as the bag was pulled off him.

'I'll fucking kill you with it,' said Jardine, his eyes screwed up, his red face hot. 'You shit insect.' And the bag was pulled from Danny. He heard the Velcro rip. The file-folders; the pads; the scratched tin box of compasses and protractors; the light-brown Valentine's card – all were spread over the carpet tiles, the tennis ball rolling unwanted among them.

It was Whieldon who saw the card. Picked it up, together with the ball. He threw the ball to Jardine but kept the card, waving it in the air. Danny shouldn't have said anything, but he heard himself doing so.

'Give it to me.'

Whieldon threw it to Jardine. Jardine read out the address. 'What's this?' he said, wafting it in the air like a fan.

'Give it to me.' Danny heard the envelope tearing. He didn't want to look. He searched his imagination for some kind of reason why the card was there – who he might be posting it on behalf of. A sick grandmother who always used to send him Valentines? It was useless. He didn't even speak as the thing was withdrawn.

'To Daniel – from question mark – with love.' The last word read out by Jardine with humiliating emphasis.

'What?' said Pickering, delighted at his own incredulity.

'To Daniel from question mark with love,' Jardine said again. 'Sending yourself Valentine's cards,' he added loudly for the benefit of others in the room.

'MacFadden's sending a Valentine to *himself*,' said Pickering.

'MacFadden, you wanker. You sad fucking wanker.'

Danny couldn't speak. He couldn't move.

'I'm in love with myself,' said Whieldon.

'What's the matter with you, you sad fucking shit,' said Jardine.

Later, sitting in economics. Mr Geldard at the front writing on the whiteboard, while from behind a gentle chorus began, almost inaudible at first, swelling gradually until it filled the room.

'With the record selection, with the mirror reflection, I'll be dancing with myself . . . I'll be dancing with myself.' Soon the whole class was singing.

'Well, there's nothing to prove and there's nothing to lose . . . I'll be dancing with myself . . . dancing with—'

Mr Geldard turned around and the class immediately silenced, all eyes flicking down to notepads and laps. All eyes except Danny's, which stared straight ahead and were wet with tears.

He was silent at dinner that night. He wasn't going to speak of what had happened. He couldn't have done had he been asked to. Everything burned inside.

'Greg's going to see the Valetta game,' said Lawrence, Danny's eldest brother.

'The jammy fucker,' said Marshall, Danny's younger brother.

'Marshall. If you don't mind,' said his father.

'Yeah, Marshall,' said Lawrence, flicking a pea at him, 'don't be such a foul-mouthed fucker.'

'Lawrence,' said his father.

Michael

'Yeah, Lawrence,' said Marshall. 'You bastard.'

Danny's father leaned across and hit Marshall's knuckles with a fork. Lawrence laughed. Danny read the back of the ketchup bottle throughout this exchange, trying to use the list of contents to force the words of the song from his head. Even when he mentally shouted it down the Gen X lyric ran on and on. Without warning Danny stood up.

'Daniel,' said his father.

'Toilet,' said Danny.

His father watched him leave the kitchen.

'You know what Greg's like,' said Lawrence, not responding to Danny's exit. 'With his luck the car'll break down, or they'll get lost on the way or his dad'll die or something.'

'Give me that potato if you're wasting it.'

'Fat pig.'

'Says you.'

'Says you.' The banter faded out as Danny made his way upstairs.

He was relieved to find himself in the bathroom. He shut the door. Felt safety and satisfaction as he slid the bolt and flicked its hexagonal arm downwards. The relief was momentary. The burning returned to his belly. He took off his shirt. He hated looking at himself. He was the wrong shape. His thinness a metaphor for his weakness. All he could discern was a skeleton. There was something repulsive about it. He examined the lines down his arms. Different shades of pink and red depending on what stage of healing they were at. They marked time. A calendar of shame. But he was proud of them too. They were his. They spoke of a certain courage. An identity. He'd already spotted the razor in the hollowed-out soap-holder dug into the tiled wall. It was at the back, behind a wodge of wet soap – a cheap yellow and white disposable. The edge of the blade was visible. It winked in the light. He didn't want to think about it, but the idea was there, upon him. A delicious thrill. Something to counter the song which persisted and bit. There was anger too, and hatred.

Some for Jardine and his pack, but more, much more, for himself. Without even being aware of reaching for it he found the razor in his hands, the imperfect steel dotted with dried soap and severed yellow hairs. He picked at the surrounding plastic. It hurt his nails. He remained determined, the sensation dulling, or shouting down the feelings of vileness – a trailer for what was to come. How far could he go? A cold rush of adrenaline. His heart thumping tightly. The blade, free now, its bared base cleaner and lighter than its sullied edge. He wanted to shout as he dug it into his arm, not in pain but with the release of it. The rage and hatred he felt for himself. For everything. Himself was everything. Let it stop. Let it cease. Let it go black and end and hate and fuck them and fuck me.

It was two months before they let him home. He must have cut deeper than he'd intended. There'd been a transfusion. Now he took to riding his bicycle around the roads that surrounded the suburban estate he lived on.

He wasn't going back to college. Not yet. Not this year. No one was going to make him. There was talk of another place, starting again. He liked the idea. The faintest tremor of interest from him brought gushes of enthusiasm from his parents. His brothers avoided him. No one was comfortable with him straying too far from home. But the bike rides were tolerated. Besides, he found he didn't want to go much further. At first he'd been nervous just leaving the house, as if there were something dangerous waiting for him outside. He imagined a thick length of pink rubber, one end looped around his leg, the other tied to a post in his bedroom. Tight at first but gradually it slackened and lengthened. The High Ashes where he lived were a thinly spread estate of sixties semis, all of similar proportion and style. But just beyond them was open countryside, some of it smeared with patches of thick messy woodland. Steadily he got to know these roads, the overgrown hedges, the pot-holed narrow lanes. He would ride back and forth, the mud-scented wind blowing sharp and cold in his face. Sometimes he would observe things. Something about the landscape attracted outsiders, or people who misbehaved. There was evidence of drug use – charred silver paper and ripped-up cigarettes. Abandoned pornography made papier mâché by the rain and dew. Sometimes he dared himself to see how late he would stay out. Not to test his parents, but rather himself. Playing with the edges of fear seemed like a new hobby. It was April and night began to fade in around seven. There was one patch of gravel opposite a field of turnips. The air was laden with their overripe pungency. On the other side of the road was a patch of woodland. It rolled down towards the A61 about half a mile away and extended ahead of him for at least twice that distance. He'd toyed with the idea of exploring it but the pink rubber wouldn't stretch that far. Once he thought he saw something stirring, deep within the unleafed branches. He stood upright on his pedals and moved off at some speed, gravel grinding beneath his wheels.

Without college and college-work to occupy him, Danny found himself cycling more and more. He rarely strayed from his adopted route although sometimes he varied the order in which he rode the roads. Inevitably he would return to the same patch of gravel. He would roll up on the bike, holding himself upright with one foot on the ground, staring into the dark mass of branches and bracken. Something kept drawing him back. It was like a dare. And then one day someone else was there. He was perturbed, as soon as he arrived, to see a figure standing, not on the gravel lay-by, but at the edge of the woods themselves. Wearing a long coat, with straight dark shoulder-length hair, their back to the outside world. Danny had to look hard to be sure it wasn't a shadow, or a misperception of tangled branches and overgrown ivy, but then the figure moved. Danny's first inclination was to ride straight off again – until he saw it was a girl of about his own age, or a little older. She stared at him. Right at him. He stared straight back. There was something combative in her gaze which he found himself determined to take on.

'Yeah?' she said.

'What?' said Danny.

'And?' she said.

'And what?' he said.

'Well, go on then.'

'Go on then where?'

'Fuck off,' she said, holding his gaze.

He stood there, his heart thudding. It wasn't fear. He wasn't going to go anywhere.

'What you doing here?' he said.

'Mind your own business.' She had stepped out of the trees, and on to the edge of the road. Danny lifted his foot off the ground and on to the pedal. He stood upright, pushing downwards, moving the bike back and forth along the gravel.

'What's in the woods?'

'Trees,' she said, holding his stare.

'Fuck off then,' said Daniel, not quite believing that he was saying it. He sat down in his saddle, pushed harder and rolled off the lay-by and on to the tarmac, speeding away from her and back towards the houses of the High Ashes. He was a little way down the lane when he heard her calling to him. He applied the brake, feeling the wheel push against its resistance. He brought the bike to a halt. He looked back over his shoulder. She was still standing there, tall and thin, outlined by the wooded undergrowth behind her.

'What is it?' he said, coming to a rest on her side of the road. He used the opportunity to gain a better view of her face. She was pretty, but pale, as if she were ill. Her dark hair was cut into a long fringe at the front. She pushed it out of her face, hooking it behind her ear.

'I said, "Have you got a light?"' She looked straight at him again, as if there were a challenge in the request.

'Don't smoke,' said Danny. The girl lifted one of her legs

and pulled at her shoe – a plain black pump. The sole was coming loose at the front. 'What's your name?' he asked. She answered him but he couldn't quite make out her reply. 'Sorry?' he said.

'Jeanne,' she said. Danny nodded. For some reason he'd thought she'd said something quite different.

They walked for a while, Danny pushing his bike ahead of him. The conversation was intermittent. Danny tried to keep it going.

'Do you know it round here?' he said.

'No.'

'Did you get the bus up – the thirty-six?' He wondered what she'd been doing. She'd walked out of the woods.

'Uh-huh.'

'Were you looking for mushrooms?' he said.

'In April?' She laughed at him, then seeing his expression said, 'Getting away from my boyfriend. He'd come looking for me.' Danny's face must have reacted in some way he wasn't aware of because she added, 'I don't like him. I never liked him.'

'Why don't you finish with him?'

'I have done,' she said, and then, after a brief pause, 'he hates me being with Michael.'

They came to a halt by a little grassy bank. It was the girl that decided to sit down. She took off her coat, laying it on the grass behind her. She shuffled backwards, seating herself on it. She was wearing a long black dress. The sleeves were loose, revealing the pale skin of her arms. They looked narrow and delicate. One finger of her hand carried a heavy-looking ring.

'Who's Michael? Your new boyfriend?'

'No,' she said, laughing. She shuffled forward as if trying to get comfortable. 'Don't want another boyfriend. Don't need another boyfriend.' She reached behind and started digging in one of her coat pockets. She withdrew her cigarettes. She flipped the top of the box revealing a lighter inside. 'I like being on my own. I like being with Michael.' Having lit a cigarette she stretched herself out, leaning back on her arms. There were three scars, hard, calloused lines of dark skin, marring the smooth cream. Cuts. She looked at Danny. Saw that he'd seen. She didn't change her posture, or try to conceal them. She drew on the cigarette and exhaled. He wondered whether to say anything. He thought about revealing his own scars. He did neither.

'You don't say much,' she said.

Danny shrugged.

'What were you doing out here?' she said.

'Nothing. I live here,' said Danny.

'Out here?'

'Over there.' He pointed down the road, towards the distant houses. He watched her smoking and was aware of feeling light-headed – almost feverish. Everything was suddenly very bright. The girl pulled on her cigarette and watched the smoke dissipating into the air.

'Do you ever think about the universe?' she said, shifting her elbows and laying on her back. She stared up at the sky. 'Shall I tell you what I like to do? I lie on my back at night and look up. But I like to imagine that this bit of the planet's facing down. So I'm looking down and down and down, into infinity.' She went quiet and closed her eyes. 'And then I like to imagine falling. And thinking that no matter how long I fell I'd never never never hit the bottom.' Danny looked at her. She turned towards him and started to laugh. She threw her cigarette, still lit, off in the direction of the trees. 'I'm joking,' she said. Then, 'Have you ever had sex?' She sat upright.

Danny shrugged. He felt uncomfortable. 'I've got to get back in a bit,' he said.

'The one thing I'd like is a good night's sleep. I used to sleep after we had sex. My old boyfriend. I can't get to sleep so easy now.'

Danny nodded.

'Do you want to know what my hobby is?' She was babbling, as if insane. In his imagination he saw the cuts, marring her skin. 'History,' she continued, answering her own question. Danny suddenly sat up himself.

'What?'

'History.'

'History's my hobby,' he said. His response sounded stupid, parroting her like a child, but it was true.

'I'll bet,' she said.

'I wrote a book about the Napoleonic wars,' he said.

'What do you mean, you wrote a book?'

'It took me three years. I started it when I was fourteen.'

'Do you know what history teaches us?' said the girl. He looked at her, waiting for her answer. 'That someone somewhere is going to set off another atomic bomb.'

Danny didn't respond. But he had had the same thought himself. The girl stood up, shaking out her coat. Again the brightness and the wooziness.

'Do you want to meet up again?' she said as she buttoned herself up.

'Meet up?' He didn't seem capable of speaking without using words she'd just used herself.

'Any time. On Monday.'

'Monday's Easter.'

'I know.' She looked at him intently. She smiled.

'All right,' he said quietly.

'Good. Two o'clock. Same place.'

'Will you be there?' he asked, hearing the foolishness of the question.

'Turn up and see.' She crossed back over the narrow road, back towards the woods. She glanced at him and then walked purposefully into them, as if they were where she lived.

The rest of the weekend Danny cycled about his adopted domain, trying not to pause every five minutes at the patch of gravel where the trees started. He'd filled an old tartan flask from the tap. He stopped at one point and sat on the small grassy bank sipping from it. He watched the branches, thinking he might see her striding out of them at any time. It was cool, cooler than when he'd set out. He pulled his duffel coat around himself. It was new. The material still felt stiff and unfamiliar. Mum had bought it for him when he came out of hospital. He swigged at the water. It tasted metallic. He wished he'd let the tap run longer, and then he remembered it was a side-effect of the tablets they'd put him on. Everything tasted like that. A gust of wind came, picking up a faded foil packet from the side of the road. It skittered around the uneven tarmac in a circular dance before being pulled along into the trees. Danny found himself on his feet. He left his bike where it was, flat against the grass. It would be all right for a few minutes. He'd never once seen anyone else here. Apart from the girl.

He supposed he'd wandered in there hoping to find the footpath – the one she must have taken down to the main road assuming that was where she had gone. He hadn't walked far before exploring any deeper became very difficult. The remains of bracken snagged his feet. Lines of narrow birch and brambles seemed to thicken with every step. One of the toggles of his coat caught on a spiralling branch of holly. He looked back over his shoulder. He could still see his bike. He had only come ten metres or so and he could get no further. She must have come from a different part of the woods. He looked around, trying to peer through the slatted undergrowth. It was thick and dark and silent. With difficulty he made his way back out into the light.

Danny sat at dinner as he had sat at every other dinner since he had returned home, watching the family around him rather than participating in their banter. Marshall – who had taken up magic as a hobby – was performing a trick with the pepper grinder, wrapping it in a paper serviette.

'You're such a prick, Marsh.'

'Shuddup.'

'I can see it's gone already.'

'Shuddup. Just watch.'

'It's in your lap. You've dropped it in your lap. There's nothing there.'

Danny watched them through a screen of thick Perspex. The only thing that was different now was that there was something with him on his side of the plastic. He was accompanied by the thought of the girl. He saw Lawrence reach across and press the paper serviette flat.

'See – told you.'

'Dad!'

'You're a faker. You're so shit, Marshall.'

Danny felt himself force another smile.

Later they were in the living room, playing Rummikub. Or rather everybody else was. Danny sat back on the sofa, looking on, watching them kneeling around the coffee table in the centre of the room shouting at each other.

'Dad. Tell him. He's putting down more than he's allowed.'

'Ignore him, Father. He knows not of what he speaks.'

'You put down a seven and thought I wouldn't notice.'

'Dan – are you coming to Marshall's magic club show?' Lawrence had turned to Danny, suddenly moving his attention from the game.

'Leave him, Lawrence,' said Marshall. 'Danny. You don't have to go.'

'I think he should go. I think you should go.' Danny, not expecting this direct engagement, shrugged his shoulders. 'Why not? It's your brother's inaugural night. The rest of us have got to suffer.'

'Leave him,' said Dad.

'I just thought he might enjoy it.'

'You can talk,' said Marshall. 'You didn't want to watch an hour ago.'

'I just thought he might want to get out the house. See some life.'

'Lawrence,' said Dad.

'Come on. It'll be a laugh. We can heckle him together.'

'No thanks.' Danny heard himself say it. Hating himself for not wanting to go. Hating Lawrence for asking him.

'Well, great. How's that for family solidarity.'

'Lawrence. Leave him alone.'

Danny stood up from the sofa. He walked towards the door.

'Danny.' Lawrence called to him. 'Danny.' Danny reached the comfort of the corridor outside and headed for the stairs.

When he set out on Monday – the bike friendly beneath him – Danny didn't expect that the girl would be there. But he rode off anyway. He wanted to see her. He'd been trying to picture her almost all the intervening time since they last met. It was the feel of her that he'd been able to recall so clearly. A sharp spike that somehow brought comfort.

It was colder today. A return to winter. The narrow branches swung and swayed. He almost didn't want to dismount. He felt that if someone were to observe him, sitting on the grassy hump in this chilly weather, they would think he was mad, or misbehaving. He stared into the woods. There was a fence at their threshold. Struts of splintered oak, roughly nailed into one another. He supposed this whole area was part of the old golf course – which was now disused, most of it sold off for building development. Only the woods remained wild and untrodden, part of something else. Did anyone own woods, or were they just there, like the sea?

'Hello.'

He turned startled. She was stood at his side.

'I didn't think you were going to come,' he said. She was dressed as she had been before. Her long coat. Her heavy ring.

'Michael wasn't going to let me. I came anyway.'

Danny nodded. He didn't like this talk of Michael. It made him tighten up. Made her feel further away from him.

'Do you want to meet him?' she said. 'I thought you might like to.'

'Maybe. If you like.' There was a pause in which Danny heard the rush of the wind through the branches. 'I thought . . . I thought you might want . . . a walk or something.' He was nervous just being with her. She seemed so much older than him. She pursed her lips, studying him.

'I thought you might want to come with me. To see where we are,' said the girl. 'No one knows you're there.'

Danny nodded again. His heart was fluttering. A tingling inside. The sense of being about to cross some line he had never dared cross before.

'Come on, then.'

As he swung his legs over the old fence Danny found himself wondering what her life must be like. Nothing like his. He wanted to ask about it but was frightened that it might anger her, that she might abandon him. He didn't want to be without her. He'd been clinging on to the thought of her for three days.

As the trees and ferns closed around them the tight-headed wooziness returned – a sense that he was somewhere to the left of his mind and body, watching what was happening with a detached eye. The feeling made him panicky and he searched for real physical details to cement himself into reality: the sensation of treading down the overgrown grass stalks; the momentary discomfort when he caught his ankle on an exposed tree root. When he'd tried to walk in here by himself he'd been unable to find a path. The girl knew her route as if it were marked clearly in the uneven ground. There was no indication that Danny could discern of when to turn one way or when to head another yet she seemed to have an unerring instinct about exactly where to go next. The tangled brambles and clumps of dried-up ferns seemed to part for her as she moved.

The further they got into the trees the more Danny's sense

of alarm grew. The idea that he wouldn't be able to find his way out of there.

'You know what,' he said. She hadn't spoken a word since they left the road. 'I think I'm going to have to head back.' She continued walking, as if she hadn't heard him. Despite himself Danny carried on walking faster, trying to catch up with her. He didn't want to be left alone in there. 'I said, I think I'm going to head back. I didn't realise it was this far.' She came to an abrupt stop and turned towards him.

'You know what, Danny,' she said. 'You've just got to make a choice. You can go back. Or you can come with me. It's completely up to you. You've just got to decide.' She looked at him directly. Danny could hear a rustling high above, the cawing of some great black bird – an unseen crow or rook wrestling with prey. She put one hand on her hip and chewed her lip waiting for his response.

'I'll come with you,' he said, and it started to rain.

The branches above them began to patter. As they walked fronds of ferns and broad-leafed weeds hopped and jerked under the percussion of the raindrops. The air itself seemed to be tinged green. Water ran down Danny's face. Momentarily, he felt submerged.

'Sometimes,' said the girl, her voice only just audible above the rush of falling water, 'sometimes do you wake up and think, How am I going to make it to the other side?'

'What?' said Danny.

'The other side of the day. Have you ever woken up and had that thought?'

It was a common thought for Danny. A regular feeling. 'No,' he said.

'Really. I thought you might have.' She strode onward, navigating the incline ahead of them without any drop in her pace. The terrain was unexpectedly dramatic. They seemed to be in some kind of gully, a former watercourse perhaps or a glacial path. Any sense of the proximity to the old golf course, now built on, had disappeared.

'But don't you find yourself thinking about the future – and not wanting it? Like something ugly someone's given you.'

'No.

She turned and smiled at him. 'Yes, you do. I know you do.'

'No, you don't.'

'When I first saw what Michael showed me, I was scared. I don't feel anything now. That's better, isn't it?'

The woods had become quieter now. The occasional bird-song had faded out, without Danny noticing. Maybe the rain had silenced them. Just the trudge of their footsteps and the swish of the vegetation as they passed.

'I never got how my parents saw the world,' said the girl. 'To them it all looked clean and safe and they thought that's how it is.'

'Things are one way underneath,' said Danny. 'Else how do you get history?'

She let out a high-pitched laugh, almost like a squawk.

'There's no such thing as history. That's made up too. The made-up things get solidified – that's all.'

'The world is as the world is,' said Danny.

'The world is shit,' she said, coming to rest in a muddy clearing. 'It hurts Danny and that's the truth. Isn't it? The world just hurts.'

'It doesn't always,' he said.

'Doesn't it? When didn't it for you?'

'Lots of times,' he said.

'Yeah. Lots of times.' She picked up a stick from the ground and began to bash away at a large fern. Drops of water flew off it, into the damp air. 'I believe you,' she said.

As they ascended towards the summit of a small hill Danny spotted something emerging through the branches – the slated roof of a small building. They rose higher and more of it emerged. It stood alone, surrounded by dark trees and foliage. It wasn't until they reached the crest of the slope that Danny became aware of something else, an obstacle between them and the structure – a large expanse of black stagnant water. It filled a portion of the valley beneath them. The ground around the circle of shore nearest them was flat and navigable but it rose abruptly on both sides forming a kind of natural funnel. The escarpments were rocky and knotted with brambles and bracken. They didn't look at all passable.

'Reservoir,' said the girl. 'It fed the golf club.'

'How do we get to there? To the building?' He assumed that was where they were going. She scrambled down the other side of the hill, until she reached the water's edge. She sat down on a small rock, gathering her coat beneath her. It had stopped raining.

'Through there,' she said. He raised his eyes to look at the water. It narrowed at the far end to a small neck only a metre or so wide. Jutting from this area was a rusted metal railing, canted at an odd angle. Wet-looking vegetation coiled around its spokes.

'You're joking,' said Danny. The girl shook her head.

'No,' she said. 'That's the way through. That's the only way through.'

'Well, I might as well head back now.' He thought about his bike, leaning on the mound of grass. The girl laughed.

'Why?'

'I'm not going in there.'

'Why?'

'It's freezing. And dirty. I don't care what's over the other side.'

'It's easy, Danny.'

'I don't care. I'm not going in.'

'I'll go first. I'll show you the way. You only have to follow me.'

'No.' He stayed where he was – halfway down the slope. She stood up, holding his gaze.

'You've come this far,' she said. 'Why wouldn't you go all the way, Danny?'

He stood there shaking his head.

'Michael's waiting.'

'No.'

'Well, he was right. He said you were a coward.'

'What?'

'He said you wouldn't want to come.'

'How does he know? He doesn't know me.'

'Playing it safe. Too fucking safe. You haven't got the guts.'

'No. That's not true.'

'Just too frightened. Too frightened to show them.'

'You don't know. He doesn't know anything. You don't know anything.'

'Well, come in then. Show them. Then they'll understand.'

'No.'

'Come on.'

'No.' Danny turned. Began to head back up the slope. Tried to imagine his way back out of the woods.

'Danny.'

'No.'

'Well, I'm going through. I'll see you,' she said.

He wasn't going to turn around.

'Say goodbye, then,' she said. The woods all vivid around him – the greens and browns, the wet earth, the rotting flora. He thought of not seeing her again. He wanted to take one more look, to fix her in his mind. To prove that he hadn't imagined the whole encounter. She was still there, at the edge of the dirty water. 'Well?' she said. Danny shook his head – the smallest movement he could bring about while still answering her question. She raised her eyebrows. He repeated his miniature headshake. Then, without any indication as to what she was doing, she shrugged off her coat. Still looking at him, she reached behind her head and began unbuttoning her dress. She stepped out of it, laying it on the ground. She slipped off her pumps and rolled down her tights. For a moment she stood there, in black underwear – a vision against the skeletal trees behind her. Danny found that he'd turned to face her, his heart skipping. She smiled and reached behind her head again, unhooking her bra. He could see the goose pimples forming on the skin of her arms, her small breasts and nipples hardening in the cold. The thickened red lines of scar tissue around her wrists. He walked towards her. He was in territory he'd never trod before. When he was about a couple of metres from her, standing level with her on the shoreline, she took off her pants.

'Come on,' she said.

He began to unlace his boots, sitting down on the dry, decaying leaves to pull them off. He was trying not to think about what would come next. He pulled at his jumper, and then the sweatshirt beneath. He felt the cold air hit his own scars, rawer and more recent than hers. He wanted her to see them, to acknowledge them. He looked at her, angling his arms towards her as he unbuttoned his jeans. Her nakedness felt like a point, digging into him. She smiled at him and he went towards her. He'd kept his own pants on. Before he reached her she turned and walked into the water. He winced at the thought of it.

'What about our clothes?' he asked. She didn't answer.

He watched her beauty, the pale gentle curves, disappearing into the black water. He felt the decision being made somewhere within. He followed her.

At first, up to his ankles, it was almost acceptable, but as he felt the line of cold climb his legs it became more like pain.

'Just do it, get your shoulders wet, get under.' She was ahead of him, swimming languorously along. The bottom of the pool fell away sharply, and the uncomfortable muddy stone was replaced by a void. Forcing himself, feeling something like exhilaration, he swam after her. The sensation didn't last. The coldness was too much. He thought it would become tolerable, but in fact it became harder to cope with as each second passed. She was at the iron gate, the rusted metalwork slimy and black where it jutted from the water. 'Come on then,' she said. 'Let's do it.' Danny began to panic. He couldn't feel anything beneath him. He pushed his legs around in the water, wanting to sense something, to prove they hadn't gone numb. They might as well have been amputated. There was only an absence – an area in which he had no effect at all. He tried to turn around in the water, but there was something like a current moving him towards the gate. There was the girl ahead of him, her dark hair spread out on the water around her. 'Deep breath,' she said.

'Don't,' said Danny.

She plunged herself under the water. Suddenly he was alone on the surface. 'Don't,' he said again but there was no way she could have heard. He was breathing very fast. Too fast. His head buzzed. Everything seemed very dark. The sense of being alone there was unbearable. In spite of the freezing water biting into him he went under. He didn't want her to leave him there.

At first he didn't think he would be able to open his eyes. It took two or three goes. When he did, there was just enough light to see. There was a sense of rippling sky above, broken by branches. It seemed lighter from down there. She was ahead of him, near the plunging black lines of the iron grille. There barely seemed enough room to swim through. He would have to turn back. He would have to return to the surface. But she was through, or she seemed to be on the other side. He reached out and touched the iron. Its surface was abrasive, full of tiny jags and splinters. A hand reached out from the other side. Her heavy-ringed hand. It pulled at Danny with some force, dragging him into the grille. He would never get through. His head might, his shoulders even, but not his hips. As he had this thought, she seemed to pull even harder. Something was wrong. Her hand was colder than the surrounding water – a blacker hole in an already black sky. He needed to take another breath. The need was transforming itself into a hurt. He thought he could see her face. He thought he could see her smile. There was nothing pleasant in it – only wickedness. He thought of the last smile he'd seen. His brother Marshall. He thought of the magic show, thought of them laughing. Thought of Lawrence, sitting next to him, squeezing his leg. He pulled back from the grille, using whatever force he could draw on. He stretched up hard, reaching down deep within himself, pulling and pulling and pulling.

He found himself on the side of the shore, curled up tight, hugging his legs. He couldn't remember how he got there. He was shivering, his teeth clicking uncontrollably, every joint tight. He propped himself up on his elbows. He could see the girl on the other side of the gate, or at least what he took to be her hair, pooling across the scum-covered surface of the water.

'Jeanne,' he called out. It was the first time he'd used her name. He waited for her to break the surface. When she didn't he called her name again. He scrambled around until he found his things, trying to dry himself on leaves and desiccated ferns as he searched. Despite the fact that he was still damp he got dressed as hurriedly as he could. He felt that he'd dreamed taking his clothes off. He tried to get as close to the gate as possible. He found a broken branch on the ground. Clinging to the earthy bank at the side of the pool, he poked the branch through the slimy ironwork. 'Jeanne,' he said again. He waited for her to grip the branch. A hand broke the surface. It was black. As black as the water. As black as the hair. At first he thought it couldn't be hers. It was swollen and fat-fingered. And then he registered, almost embedded in the purulent tissue, her heavy silver ring. He leaned across the water as far as he dared, pushing the branch. A face broke the water, or the remains of one. Half of it was consumed by a grin where the flesh had gone. The eye sockets were empty too. Only the hair remained as he had seen, thick and dark, trailing down over the exposed bone.

It was three weeks before he told anyone. It made no difference – except to her grieving parents who'd thought she had fled to London, fifteen months earlier. She'd been called Georgia.

Nobody had ever heard of Michael.

The Bear

It was in 2005, the year of his father's death, that Daniel Sher finally went to the ball. It was a biennial event his company held at the Tavern on the Green – a gaudy yet beautiful affair held at a gaudy yet beautiful location. Daniel was not a native New Yorker – he was in fact from New Zealand – but he loved Central Park and he loved the Tavern and more than anything he loved the fact that he was now a partner at Askey and Bryant and therefore invited to the Partners' Ball. He was at home, he'd found his place, the ground was solid and there he stood.

The ball was traditionally held on 11 November – Veterans Day. The original Mr Bryant had lost two sons in the Second World War and the event was established partly in their memory. For Daniel this was an inconvenience. He would have liked to pick his costume up as late as possible – given that the revelation of who was wearing what contributed much to the impression created on the night. But Tuesday was a public holiday and the store would be closed. This meant he would have to collect his outfit today and lug it to the gallery opening he was attending with Sacha that evening. Things were further complicated by the fact that he was moving into his new office. This task had to be completed, or at least meaningfully begun, by the end of the day, leaving just enough time to get to the costume store before it closed. Experience had taught Daniel to delegate anything that could be delegated – but the actual hiring of the costume he wanted to do himself, to ensure everything was as it should be. He wished he had completed the chore sooner. He had overlooked its importance. A conversation in the men's room with J.T. McNeil had convinced him that this had been a mistake.

'Sher. Partner in law. How does *that* feel?' J.T. stared down at his own stream of urine, focusing its jet into the black holes of the drain.

'Pretty good, sir, pretty good.'

'"J.T.",' said J.T., looking up briefly from his piss.

'Pretty good, J.T.' Daniel smiled as he unzipped.

'In time for the ball too. Want some advice?' J.T. shook himself vigorously, concentrating intently on the action as he spoke.

'Love it,' said Daniel.

'Make an impression.'

'Sir?'

'"J.T."'

'J.T.?'

'People will *remember* what your costume is. So choose something memorable. Make the most of that little opportunity. You get me?' He shovelled his penis back into his trousers and zipped himself up briskly.

'Thank you, J.T., I will.'

'Nothing too self-conscious. But something with wit. With taste. With balls.'

'I understand.'

'My first year as partner – I came as Judge Roy Bean. Thought I was being clever – nobody knew who I was. Which was very telling. Two years after I went as King Kong. And Charlotte was Fay Wray. Never looked back after that.' J.T. studied his reflection briefly, smoothing down a stray strand of hair. 'Bold and clear, Danny. Bold and clear.'

*

The Bear

Daniel had settled on the idea of a gladiator. His legs were strong and would look good in skirt and sandals. There was a level of fun, of irony, that would neatly disguise any macho subtext. Plus Sacha would be able to wear something suitably alluring to complement it – a short slave-girl dress, something off the shoulder that would reveal generous hints of her magnificent bust. There would be many reasons to envy Daniel, all on clear display – his youth, his vigour, his partner – virtually every aspect of his life. He stood in the corner of his new office, regarding himself in the darkening glass of the windows. The lights of Manhattan were coming on below, shining through him. What would Dad have thought of this? No way of telling him now. But he had known where Daniel was heading. He would have taken that knowledge to the grave. Daniel shook his head. Such thoughts were indecent. He had loved his father. They were different, that was all.

He walked down Lexington Avenue, savouring the crispness of the November evening. He risked a glance at his watch. He started walking faster. The store closed – eccentrically, he thought – at 5.45 p.m. There was still plenty of time.

There had never been fancy dress parties in his youth. The Sher residence was not a party house. His friends had conjurers, puppet shows, long games of cricket in the Auckland sun. What did Dad organise for him? 'Reading parties' – poetry and stories. Daniel had been ashamed. Embarrassed. Sickened at his difference from everybody else. Immersed in the university, his father could see no wrong in this version of a good time. Daniel still felt the pain – his friends sat there, more bored than they would have been on a school day as his father enunciated the *Wind in the Willows* like a Shakespearian actor.

What mattered now? What mattered was this. The reality of the broad Manhattan pavement beneath Daniel's feet, the hustle of the street, the money in his pocketbook, in his bank. The only words that touched him were the black and white type of the *New York Times* and the *Wall Street Journal.* This was Daniel's reality and he had sewn it for himself, stitch by laboured stitch.

Taking a left turn he noticed the elegance and neatness of the shopfronts start to become more chaotic, the buildings were lower, more human in scale, more like the ones he remembered from childhood. Strange. He had never thought it before and yet when he glanced up at the rooms above the awnings he was surprised to see pastel shades and little balconies – just like Mission Bay back home. He checked where he was going in his PDA. 378a Third Avenue – The Gramercy Costume and Novelty Store. He searched among the signage and the window displays – it would be quicker than looking for numbers on the chaotic, crowding doorways. 'Katie's Nails', 'The Cooperhouse Tavern', 'Something from Nothing'. There it was – a faded harlequin in the window, in between two falling packs of cards, suspended like a freeze frame from ceiling to floor. Pleased to have found it, looking at his watch again, Daniel crossed the road.

The air inside was warm. A ceiling-mounted fan heater rattled above the entrance. Daniel shut the door behind him. Somewhere, some way off, an old-fashioned bell tinkled musically. He glanced around the small premises, which seemed shabby and antiquated, though beneath his urgency Daniel perceived a dim sense of pleasure too. It was a shop he would have loved as a child – full of the kind of vulgar delights that were taboo in the Sher household. He shook his head as if to dispel a clouding thought. He didn't have time. Behind the counter was a large old man in a cardigan and check shirt. He was jowly and wet-lipped with a mess of white hair. A little black boy stood absorbed in a demonstration of a magic trick.

'Watch it. Watch it,' said the man. It sounded like a warning but he was talking to the boy.

'I'm watching it,' said the boy – sounding like he wanted to please.

The old man swirled three walnut shells around a black foam rubber mat. His age, shabbiness and the air of poverty he exuded suggested he couldn't be far from a retirement home but the skill and grace with which his fingers moved contradicted this impression quite disarmingly.

'That one,' said the boy, when the old man's fingers had come to a rest. With an emphatic gesture the old man inverted the chosen shell, revealing nothing but emptiness underneath. His old baggy face broke out into a huge smile.

'Pick again,' he said.

Daniel chose this moment to cough noisily. 'Go on,' said the old man, not reacting to Daniel's presence in any way.

Daniel looked at his watch. 'Excuse me,' he said aloud.

'Which one do you think?' said the old man, theatrically oblivious to Daniel's presence. 'Think carefully.' The little boy stared at the two remaining inverted shells, his head moving slightly as he considered one then the other.

'Excuse me—'

'We heard you already,' shouted the old man without looking up. 'We're busy.' Maybe he was shouting because he was deaf, or maybe he was just irritated. Daniel felt his own irritation rising within.

'I understand you're busy . . .' Daniel said without understanding at all. But the old man had returned his full attention to the little boy who was making his next choice.

'That one,' said the boy, content with whatever reasoning had led him there.

'Aha!' said the old man, delighted. He flipped up the shell and there was nothing beneath. 'Now which one?'

'If you don't mind – I have a—'

'We do mind.' The old man returned his attention to the little boy. 'Which one?'

'Now you're being silly,' said the little boy. He pointed to the last remaining walnut shell. 'It can only be there.'

'Well, see for yourself,' said the old man. The little boy reached out and flipped it up. Nothing but emptiness.

'No way!'

'How do you like them apples!'

'Where is it?'

'Who knows?' The old man shrugged his shoulders in an exaggerated manner.

Daniel felt he had to interrupt. 'I'm sorry but I'm going to have to insist that you serve me. I'm sure this young man won't mind.'

The old man turned his full attention to Daniel. Daniel was surprised to feel himself shrink a little.

'Pretty sure of yourself, aren't you,' said the old man.

'My assistant called earlier. I've paid a deposit on a costume.' Daniel tried to sound firm.

'Patience is a virtue. You know that, don't you,' said the old man, staring down at him like a teacher. 'Virtue is its own reward.'

Daniel didn't say anything. He took out his wallet and opened it, allowing the thick sheaf of bills within to show.

'You mind?' said the old man to the young boy, his voice noticeably softening.

'I guess not,' said the child who gave Daniel a casual glance before turning back to the counter.

'Well, maybe we can go ahead and see what the gentleman wants. Now then, sir. How may we serve?'

'My assistant called earlier. Reserved a costume. Sher's the name.'

'Sher. Sher,' said the old man, searching his memory as he spoke the surname aloud. 'Sher,' he said again which began to make it sound abstract, the repetition emptying it of meaning. 'Sher . . .'

'Sher,' said Daniel again.

'Sher. Yeah. Yeah. Gladiator, was it?'

'Gladiator. Yes.'

'Ain't got one.'

'I beg your pardon.'

'Ain't got one. Sorry.' The old man looked at Daniel unapologetically.

'I've paid a deposit.'

Without taking his eyes off Daniel the old man banged the till with his elbow. Its bell rang and the draw clunked open. He withdrew a ten-dollar bill.

'I've paid a deposit and I need my costume,' said Daniel.

'Sorry,' said the old man.

'Well, sorry won't do,' said Daniel feeling his angry inner lawyer rise to the surface. 'When you took payment we entered into a contract.'

'That right?' said the old man.

'That's right,' said Daniel. 'And contracts can't just be broken on a whim. Now I need a gladiator costume by tomorrow night and I expect you to provide me with one.'

'Expect away,' said the old man. 'Ain't got one here.'

'Well, I'm not leaving this shop until you hand it over.'

'Bully for you. Gets pretty cold in here nights when I turn that heater off. I'll see you Wednesday morning.' He slammed the till draw shut, leaving the ten-dollar bill on the counter.

Daniel tried to take charge of his rage. It was important to remain in command of the situation. If he left the shop without an outfit he would have approximately twenty minutes to find another costume store. Most such places, if not all, would be shut tomorrow. It was not a smart play to let this matter slide out of his control. He took a deep breath. 'Would you,' he heard himself say, 'would you perhaps be able to furnish me with another costume, something similar if possible?' He wasn't going to apologise. He was not in the wrong. But he hoped that he sounded reasonable enough to persuade the old man to rethink.

'Similar costume, huh?' The old man sniffed, wiped the underside of his nose with one of his thick fingers. 'What's similar to a gladiator?' he said to the little boy. 'Soldier? Knight of the Round Table?' Daniel thought for a minute. A knight would work. His legs would still look good in tights.

'A knight might be good, yes,' Daniel said, trying to let his enthusiasm show.

'Ain't got one.' The old man held Daniel's gaze.

Don't lose your temper, he thought. He's got you sized up. The old man was clever. This was courtroom thinking. Or at least poker table thinking. The proprietor knew exactly who had the power.

'Do you think I might be able to browse. Choose something for myself?' said Daniel, trying to peer over the man's shoulder, into the back of the shop.

'Browse?' said the old man as if it was the first time he'd ever heard the word. 'Browse.' He raised his eyebrows, widened his eyes, looked down at the little boy, considering the matter. Then after a moment came the reply: 'Nope. Costumes are stored downstairs. Ain't got no liability insurance for downstairs. If you were to slip on the stairs – which are pretty treacherous – well, I guess you'd be able to sue my ass off.' He looked at Daniel and sniffed noisily. 'So nope. Can't really let you browse.' There was silence for a moment. The sound of traffic rumbling outside. The hum of Manhattan winding itself up for the evening.

'Well, how might we best resolve this – the matter of me choosing? My choice? Of costume?' Another pause. The old man sniffed again.

'Well, I reckon I've got just what you need,' he said eventually, scratching his hairy neck. 'Masquerade ball, is it? Professional function.'

'Yes,' said Daniel, feeling a rising sense of panic.

'You want to make an impression, then. Something people ain't likely to forget.'

A moment and then Daniel said, 'Yes.' His only option was to surrender. At least it would be quick.

'Yep, I reckon I've got just the outfit,' said the man, smiling for the second time.

*

The Bear

The weight of the thing was extraordinary. It came in its own bespoke canvas bag. Daniel struggled back up towards Lexington Avenue, searching for the promise of a taxi light. If it was this heavy to carry – and the straps of the holdall cut into his shoulder like a blade – what would it be like to wear. Three children approached with their mother – all of them holding silver balloons. They laughed, bumping their helium-filled spheres together as they passed. They seemed oblivious to Daniel's presence, flowing around him like water around a stone. The costume would be easier to wear than to lift. The load would be spread evenly around his body. The impression created would surely be worth the pain.

At first Daniel had been disappointed. The thing looked mangy, dirty even. But the old man had brushed the fur, demonstrated the arrangement of braces and fastenings inside. Then he produced the jewelled waistcoat and decorative collar. The sense of grandeur, of specialness, of importance, was striking, offset by the uniqueness and charm of the outfit itself. Daniel's initial disappointment was replaced by a rising excitement.

'You'll need someone to help you into it.'

'I have someone.'

'And help you out. Not easy to get out once you're in.'

'That's all right.'

'You're sure now.'

'Quite sure.'

''Cos I wouldn't rent this baby out to just anyone. She needs appreciation.'

'I understand.'

'From Russia. And before that Budapest. Very old. Made by gypsies.'

'I understand.'

'You promise to look after her.'

'You have my credit card. Take what deposit you like.'

'It ain't a matter of money. This here's something special. A one-off.'

'She'll be back Wednesday morning. First thing.'

'First thing, you say.'

'Yes.'

The old man studied Daniel for a moment, clearly thinking. Whatever it was he was thinking about remained inscrutable.

'Take her, then,' he said after a moment. '*Geh gesund a heit.*'

Daniel arrived in Chelsea fifteen minutes late. The traffic was ghastly and he decided to walk the last two blocks to the gallery even though he had the costume to carry. He got there exhausted, sweating and overheated, despite the cold November evening.

'Where've you been?' said Sacha rushing towards him across the polished floor. She was immaculate as always. In his dishevelled state he felt immediately disadvantaged.

'Come on,' she said. 'I want you to meet Tobin.'

'I just need to stash this.' He tried not to sound out of breath.

'The costume?' She looked at the ridiculously large bag. 'Jesus! Have you got the chariot in there as well?' He didn't yet want to reveal that he was no longer a gladiator. He'd already had thoughts about how to address the matter of her outfit. With a change of hairstyle and some creative accessorising it would not be hard to transform her into a gypsy maid to his performing bear.

When they got the thing home – and it took both of them to carry it into the apartment from the taxi comfortably – they laid it down on their generously-sized double bed. Together they unbuckled the straps on the carry case, rolled back the canvas and revealed the costume. Sacha turned on the overhead lights in order to appreciate its splendour fully. The fur was a very dark brown, almost black. It did not look fake, more like the coat of a real animal. It exuded a faint smell, not unpleasant, but sharp and pungent: a touch of straw, a hint of earth. Though empty, the costume had bulk and form. Its arms and paws rose from the bed, its snout extended, higher than the pillows, its small ovoid ears were pricked erect. Its mouth contained teeth and a plump sculpted tongue, the glazed claws looked like they could scratch a wound in skin. Most impressive was its scale. The thing must have been nearly seven feet from toe to ear. Its feral nature was offset by the delicate and elaborate clothing it sported. The jewelled golden waistcoat and the embroidered floral collar were both exquisite pieces of work. Sacha reached down to touch the material with her fingers.

'It's old,' said Daniel, gazing down.

'How old?' said Sacha.

'He didn't know. He said various owners had added to it over the years.' The evident craft on display did indeed seem to transcend many individual lifetimes.

Sacha fingered a line of tiny ceramic hearts strung with inverted crucifixes that hung across the left breast.

'You're going to make an impression in this.' Daniel nodded and smiled. He couldn't recall having seen a costume as extraordinary anywhere.

It took them both some time to work out how to get into it. The whole thing was constructed so that when viewed from the outside there were no seams, joins or zippers visible. The illusion of a living breathing animal was complete. All fastenings were fixed internally. The heavy head itself unscrewed, like the lid of a jar. Once within it the occupant would be unable to release himself, however. There were two small latches that had to be unclipped, buried in the fur, a difficult task even with the full use of one's fingers.

Inside they found a complex series of braces, fully adjustable to adapt the costume to the size and stature of whoever was wearing it.

'Look how beautifully it's made. You can tell it's old.'

'Built to a value – rather than a cost,' said Daniel. A phrase his father used, when talking about architecture.

'Wow!' said Sacha. She drew an elegant painted nail over one of the buckles. Daniel leaned closer. There were inscriptions etched into the metalwork.

'What do they say?'

Sacha studied them. She shook her head. 'I don't know if they're words.'

'What then?'

'Runes? Hieroglyphics?' She let the buckle go, began working at the fastenings.

In the end they managed to get Daniel into it by laying the whole thing on the bathroom floor. He rolled on to his front and Sacha fastened the tiny series of buttons that ran from the waist to the neck, securing the strip that covered them with its countless inlaid hooks and eyes. They stood him up, then sat him down on a plastic stool in order to put on the head. Four complete turns fixed it in place. Daniel raised a paw and stood erect. He was now the bear.

'Oh yes!' said Sacha. 'We like. We like.' She encouraged him to walk a few steps towards her. He moved, haltingly at first, then with more confidence. It was heavy, but something about the design of the buckles and the straps, the way they distributed the load, made the weight bearable. Sacha led Daniel to the mirror. Although his field of vision was reduced he could see well enough through the band of gauze in the bear's neck. He stood in front of the mirror and admired himself.

'Magnificent,' he said, the word dull and loud in his ear.

'Is that . . . Daniel? Daniel Sher?' The word had got round already. Low music filtered in through the gauze at the front and at the back (a separate patch, lower down, had been included for the purposes of ventilation.) Daniel raised a paw. He found the laughter and wonder that the costume was unfailingly being greeted with truly gratifying. His gladiator wouldn't have warranted much more than a wry smile. Besides there were several soldiers, and more than one of the younger partners was exposing muscled torso and legs. But there was nobody, or nothing to compare with the glory of the bear. 'Bold and clear,' J.T. had said and the bear was both. King of the skins, but refined, with a touch of European mystique, it displayed a certain witty sense of irony without descending into mere kitsch. Nobody would forget this debut. He walked carefully through the Tavern on the Green's Crystal Room managing, just about, to slip carefully between chairs and tables so as not to dislodge any plates or drinks. Sacha was waiting for him at the bar. They had worked out how to get a drink in him without having to remove the head – using conjoined drinking straws. The plan was to wait until dinner before revealing Daniel within. He wanted to avoid taking in too much liquid anyway – just enough to keep him hydrated. Urination was not a plausible option.

Here was Mr Bryant Junior – 'Herb', as Daniel was now entitled to call him. He felt something like pride rising within, that they might have a natural moment together, unsought by Daniel, yet surely inevitable. Who could pass the bear and not say something?

'I hear that Daniel Sher's somewhere in there?'

'Good evening, Herb.' He felt his heart race, but why shouldn't he use the name. That was the truth of his position now.

'Excellent show, excellent show. Just what we want to see from the new blood.' He felt a hand patting the bear's shoulder. 'Your only problem now,' said Mr Bryant Junior, smiling winningly, 'is what an earth to wear in two years' time.'

'Thank you,' said Daniel. His gratitude was heartfelt.

Daniel's plan was to make it to a row of seats he had spotted in the Terrace Room, just to have a few moments' rest before going on to Sacha. The costume was heavy, and though the bracing was comfortable, he was beginning to feel a strain in his calves and his upper back, pain in muscles that were receiving unfamiliar exertion.

'Sher!' An enthusiastic cry from a Phantom of the Opera – its face divided by a white plastic mask. It was hard to associate the chin and lips with anyone he knew. The mouth leaned close to his gauze – muttered these words – 'You are an embarrassing Kiwi prick. An embarrassment to this firm.' The Phantom was gone. Daniel felt the sting of the approbation. He hadn't anticipated it. Hadn't been able to steel himself. He stumbled on, the weight of the bear pressing down like a hand – on his head, on his shoulders, on his spine. Many smiles loomed in at him. He caught a glimpse of his own gypsy splendour in a floor to ceiling mirror. Sacha had fashioned him a small turban out of a silk scarf. There were the chairs up ahead. The heaviness was part of him now – had found its way into him. Suddenly it was becoming impossible to bear. He had to sit down.

The spot was quiet. Set back from the fray. He was weary. Everything looked distant – the lights diffused by the heavy black gauze. He sat back, grateful for the support of the chair though still feeling the weight in his shoulders, in his neck. The Tavern's famous topiary was visible from here. King Kong stood arms aloft between two streetlamps. The glittery lights twinkled, making star patterns in front of his eyes. The night was cool and clear. It looked like it would be fun just to walk among the greenery on the edge of the park, examine the animals carved from hedges, take a carriage ride perhaps, stroll unburdened in the crisp fresh air. This was not an option for him. People continued to admire the bear as they passed. The air in the costume seemed to compress. He felt the heat of it pressing against his eyes.

At 9.00 p.m. dinner was announced. Guests began to make their way to the Crystal Room, some who came via the Terrace Room had to step over Daniel's legs. Sacha found him slumped slightly, leaning against a plaster column.

'I thought you were coming to find me,' she said, holding a glass from which jutted an elongated straw. Daniel said nothing. 'Do you want a drink before we go in? Or shall we wait until we've got your head off?' She looked down at him. He was very still. Was he asleep? She wouldn't be surprised. He'd been working very hard. This event was the apotheosis of everything he'd been pushing towards his whole life. She rapped gently on the fierce heavy head. 'Daniel?' He didn't respond. 'Daniel!' she shouted through the gauze. The bear didn't move. Now she began to feel a little hook of panic, tugging at her gut. 'Daniel!' She shook the costume, lifting a weighty arm but there was no response. She released the paw and it dropped loosely against the wall. Trying to control her fingers, Sacha reached round the neck, searching for the little securing latches. Having done so she twisted at the head, holding on to the ears like handles. 'I'm coming in, honey,' she said, swivelling the great hairy helmet as fast as she could.

Nothing prepared Sacha for what she found inside. Which was nothing. The costume was empty, the buckles still buckled, the fastenings still tight – the little hand-sewn label that said 'Gramercy Costume and Novelty Store' now visible, just below the neck.

At first Sacha assumed this was a joke, an elaborate joke that Daniel must have arranged with a friend from work. But in her heart she knew this couldn't be the case. There was no one Daniel was close enough to with whom he could have made such an arrangement.

Daniel Sher was never seen again. In the end – after enough time had passed, that is – nobody minded, despite Sacha's protestations. Certainly in the short term there was activity, distress, the appearance of concern. But after not too long a time Daniel Sher became another of the city's missing persons – assumed to have wandered off to some other life, some other place, until a corpse was found to prove otherwise, which it never was. Sacha disputed this version for quite a long time – after all, she knew there was no way out of that costume, not without someone else's help. And no one else had helped. But even Sacha let it go in the end. Life hummed on. And the ancient bear went back to the Gramercy Costume and Novelty Store, down to the uninsured basement, where it hung on a rail in its bespoke canvas bag.

It still hangs there today.

Acknowledgements

I am grateful to the following for their help, support and general encouragement:

My editor Antonia Hodgson particularly for her steady, unswerving enthusiasm, my agent Simon Trewin, Ra Page at Comma Press, Saurabh Kakkar at Granada.

I'd also like to thank Simon Rosenberg, Emily Senior and Iain Hunt for reading the manuscript and offering useful suggestions.

Extra big thanks to Hannah Berry for agreeing to provide her wonderful illustrations.

Finally I'm indebted to my old friend and tutor Dr Peter Millican for allowing me to use his elegant refutation of Anselm's ontological argument in 'Bound South'. I can assure readers that any flaws they may find are a result of my bowdlerisation and are not present in Peter's argument – which I've taken from lecture notes he gave to me in 1987.